HARBOUR OF LOVE

Harbour Of Love

by

Sheila Spencer-Smith

Dales Large Print Books
Long Preston, North Yorkshire,
BD23 4ND, England.

British Library Cataloguing in Publication Data.

Spencer-Smith, Sheila
    Harbour of love.

    A catalogue record of this book is
    available from the British Library

    ISBN   978-1-84262-665-8 pbk

First published in Great Britain in 2000
by D C Thomson & Co. Ltd.

Cover illustration © Heidi Spindler by arrangement with
P.W.A. International Ltd.

The moral right of the author has been asserted

Published in Large Print 2009 by arrangement with
Dorian Literary Agency

Dales Large Print is an imprint of Library Magna Books Ltd.

Printed and bound in Great Britain by
T.J. (International) Ltd., Cornwall, PL28 8RW

CHAPTER ONE

Stephanie's flowing hair skimmed the water as she leaned out of her sailing dinghy. She gasped, laughing, at the salty taste of the splashing waves full in her face. Far behind her, the Cornish coast was a thin line. She was alone on the grey sea, with the satisfying smack of sea against hull and seagulls screaming overhead.

Wasn't this worth getting up early for this morning? Yes, oh, yes! She had nearly forgotten the joy of wind and waves after months of working up in London. To think that she had even considered selling her boat.

'You without a boat!' Millie had exclaimed, glaring at her niece with the mock-angry look that was so typical of her. 'Don't talk nonsense, girl!'

Stephanie was glad now that she had

allowed Aunt Millie to persuade her to keep it. Overhead, the bright sail raked the early morning sky. Faint mist lingered above the village that was fast becoming visible as she got closer again. Her aunt's guesthouse, Harbour Spur, stood out startling white above the harbour. Stephanie had known and loved it since her earliest childhood because Millie had provided a loving home for herself since her babyhood. And in all those years she had never known anything to get her down until these recent ugly rumours started flying. Wasn't Millie due for a bit of help in the crisis that she was convinced was looming?

'They say it's true, Steph,' Millie had told her over the phone. 'The Rosslyons are selling the village.'

'They're what? Selling the village!'

A shiver of apprehension slid down Stephanie's spine.

'But how can they sell a village without telling anyone?'

Apart from Harbour Spur itself, the Rosslyon family had owned Polmerrick for generations. But no-one could buy a whole village, could they? Speculators, developers? It was clear that her aunt's livelihood would be under threat if it was allowed to happen.

'It seems they can do what they like,' Millie said, a quiver in her voice. 'Nick hasn't said anything?'

Stephanie knew her aunt would never have mentioned Nicholas Rosslyon's name in normal circumstances. She had taken a swift breath, surprised that the mention of Nick's name still had power to hurt.

'I haven't seen him for ages, Millie, since the Rosslyon Christmas Ball.'

Not since the devastating shock of his engagement to someone else, she thought.

The intervening miles between London and Polmerrick felt like oceans. Stephanie heard a deep, gasping breath on the other end of the line, and knew at once what she must do. Her help was needed at Harbour Spur. The London agency she worked for provided temporary secretaries for clients from abroad. It was interesting work and

Stephanie enjoyed it, but it could not compare with protecting Polmerrick from the hands of a developer.

Deep in thought now, Stephanie let the tiller slacken. The next moment, a gust of wind wrenched it from her hand. She succeeded in keeping the mast out of the rushing water, but was too late to prevent the boat crashing towards the beach in a welter of flaying sails. She struggled, spluttering, to her feet. The sudden easing of the boat's weight as she heaved it clear nearly had her fall over again. She steadied herself, and then stood frozen by surprise.

She had thought she was alone, and so the broad-shouldered man holding on to the other side of her boat had her mouth dropping open in amazement. The breath seemed to leave her body and then rush back like a tidal wave. The brightening sunlight showed the angles of a strong-boned face beneath dark, wavy hair. A dangerous face, she thought in that first startled moment. An unforgettable face, with condemnation in his gaze.

'We need to get the boat farther above the waterline,' he said in a deep voice that seemed to invite no argument, not that she would have given him any in the weak, exhausted state she was in.

'Thanks,' was all she could manage to gasp as they rested the boat on the shingle.

Then she stood upright, trembling now with shame at her clumsy landing. There was something about this man that emphasised her weakness. He made no attempt to move, but stood looking at her in a way she found unnerving. She reached into the boat, and tried to release the main sheet with fingers like jelly.

'Allow me,' he said.

With a swift movement he had it free, and the sail crumpled into an untidy heap.

'You timed it well,' she said shakily. 'I'm grateful.'

He laughed, and she straightened, looking up at him defiantly. He was a tall man, and the cream jacket he wore accentuated the broadness of his shoulders. It also gave him an air of authority. He held himself firmly, and she saw that the expression in his eyes as he gazed down at her held amusement now as well as censure. She took a deep breath, and then let it out slowly. All right, so she had made a mess of coming in. Until then her handling of the boat had been superb. No way was this smartly-dressed stranger going to sap her confidence.

'Should you be out on your own in such a flimsy thing?'

His voice was pleasantly deep, with a slight accent – American? But his words struck into her with a sharpness that stung.

'Flimsy?' she bit back at him.

'And you're wet through. Get yourself changed before you catch cold.'

The nerve of the man! She unzipped her lifejacket with a snap.

'The boat first. I can wait.'

The amusement in his eyes was still there.

'I'll keep guard while you change.'

Surely he didn't mean here and now? She

gave a gasping giggle, and then felt herself flush.

'It doesn't take long to get the boat sorted out. And now if you don't mind...'

He nodded his dark heard at the launching trolley farther up the beach.

'Yours?'

Immediately he crunched across the shingle to fetch it, pulling it back after him like a piece of light driftwood. His eyes were still smiling, and there was a little quirk at the side of his mouth. Stephanie was in no mood for humour. Hastily she placed her hands in readiness on one side of the craft as he did the same on the other. The boat seemed to spring into the air with the force of his grip, and then settle on to the trolley.

'It's all right. I can manage now.'

Pulling off her bulky lifejacket, she dumped it in the boat. She hoped he would take the hint and go, but as she caught hold of the trolley handle he did, too. Together they hauled it across the beach and up the slipway. Once in its usual place by the railings, the boat seemed to settle itself as if happy to be back on dry land again. Stephanie shook her dripping hair, and pushed it back behind her ears.

'It's all right. That's all that's necessary,' she snapped.

She shivered, anxious now to pack up and get home to change into dry clothes. But he wasn't listening. She shot an appraising look at him and saw that he was studying her launching trolley with a thoughtful expression on his tanned face. A holidaymaker? Not in those clothes. It was too early in the day for people to be about yet. So what was he doing here?

He turned to her, the full power of his personality shining now from his vivid blue eyes, as he said, 'D'you go out much in this thing?'

He indicated the boat with a movement of his dark head, but his eyes didn't leave her face.

'It's surprising you're not shattered by that hair-raising experience.'

She looked at him in suspicion. Was he making fun of her? The muscles in her limbs ached, and her face felt stiff with wind and salt. But shattered? Of course not. It would take more than that to shatter her.

'I've been sailing since I was born,' she flung at him, her lips tightening as she gathered up the sail.

He turned to stare at the harbour and at the narrow, iron footbridge that spanned the lock at the entrance. What could possibly interest him there? The tide was only just on the turn. There was no chance of any boats coming in or going out for some time. She cleared her throat, and the sound of it seemed to bring him back from whatever strange thoughts held him. His eyes narrowed.

'A marina is needed here for small boats like this. And bigger ones, too, of course.'

Surprised, she stared at him.

'It would make a big difference to have somewhere more suitable for launching and coming back in. It's too haphazard for a small craft like yours.'

Stung by his criticism, she stared at him with her arms full of sail.

'I got it wrong, that's all. The wind changed when I wasn't expecting it.'

He turned to her, raising a quizzical eyebrow.

'But wouldn't it be better to have improved landing facilities? For proper boats, I mean, not only things like this.'

She flushed at his critical tone.

'There's nothing wrong with my dinghy. This class of boat is popular round here.'

'Because there are no adequate facilities for anything better?'

The blood flew to her face again.

'I've had this dinghy for years, and sailed her in far worse conditions. And now excuse me. I've things to do.'

He didn't move. Instead he stood regarding her steadily, his face serious. Short of pushing him out of the way, she could do nothing but glare at him furiously.

'So, you're an expert? You sail yourself?'

she flung at him.

He shrugged, and then moved slightly to let her past.

'Not in anything as frail as this.'

'So who gives you the right to criticise what we do here in Polmerrick?'

She dumped the sails out of the way, and reached for the canvas cover. As she threw it over the boat and began to fasten it a dreadful suspicion entered her mind.

'You're not … you can't be…'

For a moment she stood quite still. So those ugly rumours of a take-over of the village really were true. Until now there had been a faint glimmer of hope that Millie's informants had got it wrong. In silence she dealt with the last fastening on the cover, and picked up the sail and her lifejacket. She felt so cold inside.

'Thank you for your help,' she managed to say.

At once he swung round.

'Don't misunderstand me. I intended no criticism. There'll be no more trouble for you coming into shore when my plans are complete.'

'There was no trouble,' she said through dry lips. 'I told you, I misjudged conditions.'

He was gazing now at the white front of Harbour Spur where the colourful hanging baskets brightened the wall. Suddenly Stephanie could bear no more. With her arms full she marched towards her home, her head held high. She didn't know if he watched her, but the back of her neck tingled. It took the strongest willpower not to turn her head as she ran up the stone steps at the side of the building. It was a relief to get inside, and crash the door shut behind her.

The sound resounded along the passage as she carried the sail and lifejacket through to the kitchen at the back. Placing the stopper in the deep sink, she turned the cold tap full on. As the water gushed, she thought of the invigorating spray on her face as she had flown across the bay, filled with the determination to do all in her power to save

Polmerrick. Was her fight going to be defeated before it began? She had a swift vision of the man she had left standing by the harbour wall – not an easy man to cross.

Turning off the tap, she plunged the sail in. She rammed it well down into the water to rid it of the salt as if by so doing she could get rid of the threat to the village, too. At last, leaving the sail to soak, she wiped her hands dry and went into the guests' dining-room at the front of the house to take a swift look through the window.

Yes, he was still there. He'd crossed the narrow bridge and was standing with his dark head thrown back, looking this way. Standing well back so he shouldn't see her, she gazed out of the window. What did he intend to do next, standing there in his cream jacket and smart trousers? He looked as out of place as a gleaming cabin cruiser would against the old fishing vessels that used the harbour. But he hadn't hesitated to come to her aid when she needed it. There had been no thought then that his light

19

clothes would get covered in tar from the beach, or that his polished shoes be stained with salt water. So what was he doing here dressed like that?

After a while, she shrugged her stiff shoulders and returned to the kitchen. She dealt quickly with the sail, and had just piled it into the basket to carry outside when there was a sound at the door. She swung around.

'Millie?'

Her aunt came into the kitchen with an early-morning tea tray from one of the guest bedrooms. Her step was light, and her denim skirt and white tea shirt gave her a youthful appearance. She looked at Stephanie in concern.

'You look as white as a sheet, Steph. And you're soaking wet, girl.'

Stephanie tried to smile but a weak grin was all she could manage. She felt it stretch the corners of her mouth.

'I've been out for a sail,' she said faintly.

'Tell me another.'

Millie Polgrean, at fifty-nine, was still a

handsome woman. Her back was as straight as a girl of twenty and there was hardly a grey hair among the brown on her erect head. What kept her young was hard work, she told anyone who asked. She had no time to waste prettying herself, or wondering where the years went. She placed the tray on the table.

'You all right, Steph?'

'The wind got up.'

Stephanie hoisted up her heavy load, and held the basket balanced on one hip.

'I'll get this lot outside on the line and then change.'

'Rough out there, was it?'

'And how,' Stephanie said fervently.

But it hadn't been as rough as her encounter back on shore. She quaked inwardly at the memory as she made a move towards the outside door. Millie put down the teapot she had taken off the tray, and looked at her suspiciously.

'So, what happened?'

'What do you mean?'

'A rough landing, too, wasn't it?'

Stephanie attempted to laugh but didn't make a very good job of it.

'I can't hide anything from you, can I? I lost concentration.'

'Obviously. I saw you from the window. I've never known you do that before, Steph. Here, give me that. I'll get that lot on the line for you.'

She made to take the basket but Stephanie swung it out of her reach.

'You've enough to do with the guests' breakfasts.'

Millie shrugged her shoulders as she set about clearing the rest of the things from the tray.

'You're a stubborn piece, d'you know that? All the same it's good to have you back for the weekend, Steph.'

'It's great being back, Millie.'

She would tell her later about her decision to stay for good.

'And the sail really was terrific. Remember all those times when I used to sail across to see Dinah?'

Stephanie smiled as she thought of her old schoolfriend's remote cottage perched on the edge of the beach across the bay, where she now worked as an artist. Dinah's place was always in a mess, and she herself looked as if she hadn't combed her flowing hair for weeks or given a thought to the clothes she threw on each morning. Dinah loved to see her, and there was always a huge welcome when she turned up unexpectedly.

Maybe she'd get a chance to sail across to see Dinah again soon now she was back for good. She was still smiling as she went outside. She slung the sail over the line and pegged it in position. Then, and only then, did she think of getting into dry clothes. She ran lightly up the first flight of stairs, pausing as usual on the wide landing to gaze at the portrait on the wall opposite. Her grandmother gazed back at her, with the suspicion of a smile in her grey eyes so like her own. Pausing here on the landing had become a ritual with her over the years.

Tamar Trevarrick, her grandmother, and Millie's mother – how lovely she looked, so calm and fulfilled. She had been painted when she was twenty-three, exactly Stephanie's own age, by a quayside artist who had caught her noble expression for ever on the canvas before him. No-one had known who he was, and the portrait was unsigned. Not that it made the slightest difference to the young Stephanie who had delighted in gazing at this grandmother she had never known.

What would Tamar Trevarrick have made of this latest threat to Polmerrick? Stephanie hesitated for a moment before walking slowly up the remaining stairs. The threatened take-over was the most direct threat to its survival that the village had ever known. And behind it, she was sure, was the mysterious, broad-shouldered man who had appeared so miraculously at the very moment she had come crashing to shore. An in whom, she had to confess, she felt more than a stirring interest.

CHAPTER TWO

Back in her room after a quick shower, Stephanie reached for her towel. Rubbing her hair vigorously, she peered out through the small window set deep into the wall. The strengthening sunshine had chased off the mist. Sunlight bathed the colour-washed buildings on the other side of the harbour. No-one stood near the harbour wall, and her stir of disappointment surprised her. Surely she didn't want to see Polmerrick's suspected enemy lurking there still?

Downstairs, Millie had their own breakfast ready on the kitchen table. She was pouring coffee as Stephanie slipped into her seat. Her aunt's face was pale, and there were the beginnings of dark smudges beneath her eyes. Stephanie looked at her in concern.

'Didn't you sleep well last night, Millie?

I've got three large suitcases in my car. I'm not going back to London, you know. I've come home for good.'

'What do you mean, girl, home for good?'

'You need my help, with this new threat hanging over Harbour Spur.'

'I'm not having you ruining your life.'

'It's done, Millie. I've made up my mind.'

The older woman turned her head away for a moment, and busied herself with clearing some crumbs from the table. As she turned back there was a suspicious glint in her eyes.

'There's more than meets the eye in this. That man I saw with you on the beach, who was he?'

To her dismay, Stephanie felt warmth flood her cheeks.

'Millie. Sit down and have something to eat,' she said.

To Stephanie's surprise her aunt obeyed.

'So, Stephanie Polgrean, you found something out from that man?' she persisted.

Stephanie picked up her coffee cup and

26

gazed at it. In her mind she saw him on the slipway with his head thrown back as he viewed Harbour Spur. It had angered her that he seemed as if he was already formulating plans for its improvement, and the village, too.

'He mentioned a marina.'

'A marina?'

Millie slapped her hand down on the table, rattling the china.

'Did he tell you his name, and whom he worked for?'

'Be reasonable, Millie. I didn't get the chance to ask.'

'Reasonable? What can be more reasonable than finding out why he's nosing about Polmerrick? I'll get on to my solicitor at once.'

'Sit down, Millie, please. It's too early yet.'

This time her aunt ignored her and started piling plates with a determined clatter.

'The place will change out of all recognition. All noise and mess when our guests come here expecting peace and quiet.'

'I'll phone Nick Rosslyon later and ask him outright,' Stephanie suggested.

Millie shot her a keen look as she took her empty plate from her.

'Maybe it's best. I'll get the guests' breakfast started, if you clear up this lot. The rooms are ready for the people coming in today.'

As Stephanie began on the clearing up she found her mind still filled with the vision of the man on the beach. But whatever happened she had work to do and nothing was going to stop her from giving it her full attention. All the same she couldn't resist a quick look out of the front window at the harbour. He wasn't there, of course. She hadn't expected it, but again she felt an odd disappointment. This was absurd, she told herself.

When the guests had finished breakfast Millie herself went on the telephone to her solicitor. Stephanie left her to it, and made herself useful in the kitchen for the second time. She had just finished unloading the dishwasher when the back door was pushed open by the bulky figure of Mrs Luke, her aunt's mainstay for the past ten years.

'You've seen him then?'

Mrs Luke thumped her shopping bag down on the draining board as she spoke, and took a flowered apron from the peg behind the door.

'You landed at his feet on the beach, so I do hear.'

How did that spicy piece of news get round so quickly, Stephanie wondered.

'What's your aunt say about it then? Not much, I'll warrant,' Mrs Luke went on.

'I caught a change of wind at the wrong moment, that's all.'

'That wasn't my meaning, as well you know.'

The door opened again and Millie came rushing in.

'That fool of a man can't tell me anything. Call himself a solicitor! He doesn't care a rap what happens to Polmerrick.'

'Calm down, Millie,' Stephanie said. 'We'll

find out for sure from somewhere else.'

Mrs Luke reached for some cleaning fluid inside the cupboard.

'Sooner than you think. I saw him not a minute since. A fine, upstanding chap if I may say so, as polite as they come. He said he'd booked in here, and would be along presently as soon as he's collected his baggage.'

'What? That man?'

Millie stared at her open-mouthed.

'Just let him show his nose in here and see what he gets! His booking's cancelled as from this minute. I shall tell him so myself.'

She marched into the hall for the reservation book that stood on the hall table beside the telephone. Stephanie followed, and read the entry over her shoulder.

'Adam Hardwicke. The only single booking,' she said aloud.

'That's him,' Millie answered and picked up a pen and slashed a thick line across the entry.

'Hey, wait a minute. There might be some mistake.'

'No mistake,' Millie said grimly.

'I'll ring Nick. Let's get the facts straight.' Millie nodded.

'No harm in that. Use the phone in my room, Steph.'

She left the bedroom door open. No privacy was needed for what was merely a business call. She dialled the familiar number, and then stood facing the open door, keying herself up for the sound of Nick's voice that had once sent flutters through her heart. The ringing tone continued for what seemed ages before the receiver at the other end was lifted.

'Charlotte Rosslyon. May I help you?'

His mother! Stephanie cleared her throat.

'This is Stephanie Polgrean. How are you, Mrs Rosslyon?'

'Oh, my dear, how lovely to hear your voice. I've been out of touch with everything for so long. And now, here I am, all alone.'

'So Nick isn't there?'

'Who?' she said with a wheezy gasp.

'I'd like to speak to Nick, if I may.'

'But Nicholas isn't here.'

'Will he be back soon? I can phone later.'

'Come and see me, dear. I'd love to see you again. Nick isn't home yet.'

'Of course I'll come and see you,' she promised.

Mrs Rosslyon had been kind to her in the past even though frequent asthmatic attacks often left her exhausted.

'This afternoon, dear, as early as you like. I've something important to tell you that I can't say over the phone.'

Stephanie replaced the receiver. She would go up to Rosslyon House to see Nick's mother, both for Mrs Rosslyon's sake and to hear from her own lips what Nick intended to do about Polmerrick. She jumped as the front door bell echoed through the house. Mrs Luke's heavy tread sounded ominous to her as Stephanie ran down the stairs to join her in the hall as she banged shut the heavy door.

'The postman.'

Mrs Luke placed a small packet on the hall table.

'No good will come of being so jittery, m'dear. What will be, will be.'

Stephanie picked up the mysterious packet.

'From Canada, addressed to this Adam Hardwicke.'

She looked at the older woman.

'I'm sure he's the man, and so's Millie. Did you notice his accent when he spoke to you, Mrs Luke? I thought it was American, but it could have been Canadian. It sounds as if we're right.'

'Right nothing.'

Mrs Luke took a duster from her apron pocket and flicked it over the telephone.

'Wait and see what happens, I say. A nice enough fellow I thought, whatever he plans to do with the place.'

'Suppose the new owner puts your cottage rent up, or tries to get you out?'

Mrs Luke shrugged.

'The Rosslyons have always been good to

us, but now Sir John's gone...'

'But surely Nick sees things the same.'

Mrs Luke drew her thick brows together. She didn't have to say more. Hadn't Nick Rosslyon sold off his father's stable of horses already? Stephanie gave a little sigh, and Mrs Luke looked at her kindly.

'Don't take on so, m'dear. A change might be good for the place, blow a little fresh air into it. Who knows? Nothing stands still, and I mustn't either or your aunt'll be after me.'

'Where is she, d'you know?'

'Out at the back somewhere, drawing up a plan of attack against that nice young man, I shouldn't wonder.'

Stephanie smiled briefly, in no mood for joking. So sure was she in her heart that they had reached the right conclusion that she had to remind herself that they wouldn't know for certain until this afternoon. She found her aunt in the back garden, pegging tea towels on the line.

'So, what did Nick have to say?'

'He's not at home. I'm to go and see his mother after lunch. Now what can I do here?'

'There's a shopping list on the kitchen table. I don't want to leave the house until after that Hardwicke man shows up.'

'You'll be careful what you say?'

'Careful! What can he do to me, I'd like to know?'

Stephanie hesitated. Somehow she knew he wouldn't take a last-minute cancellation on their part without a fight, but it was no good saying so. She turned to go indoors.

'There's a parcel for a Mr Adam Hardwicke on the hall table,' she threw back over her shoulder.

'The cheek of the man! He's not even here, yet. Well, he'll get what's coming to him, you can be sure of that, Stephanie.'

Stephanie smiled as she walked up the road away from the harbour to the shop that did service as a post office as well. She picked up a basket, and moved along the shelves with the list in her hand. It didn't take long to find the things Millie wanted. Emerging into the sunlight once more she walked down the road among a throng of holidaymakers carrying beach bags and wind breaks.

Out at sea, the sunlight played on the shimmering water. Two boats were at the quay on the other side of the narrow harbour, waiting for the high tide to push the lock gate flat on the sea bed so they could leave. This action of the tide enabled the sea-going vessels to come in and out for the space of about an hour in every twelve. A yacht, sails furled, approached the harbour entrance, and then came, under power, past the arm of the harbour wall.

Stephanie watched entranced as the yacht eased its way in. *Sea Sharon* was the name painted in gold lettering on the white hull. The vessel came slowly to rest against the quayside down below. She leaned on the rail to watch as one of the crew jumped ashore to tie up. A dark head appeared at the hatchway. A moment later a hulk of a man stood on deck, clad in blue sailing cagoule and white jeans. Beneath was a yellow shirt that caught the sunlight as he pulled off the cagoule and thrust it carelessly aside.

She recognised him at once. He held his head high as he surveyed the harbour with his hand shading his eyes. Gone was the smart appearance of the early morning. In its place was casual elegance. He called something to his companion, and bounded ashore, leaping up the slipway to the road in seconds. His vitality and obvious sense of purpose made him stand out among the crowd. He seemed primed for action, and she had a very good idea what that was.

To her surprise he turned away from Harbour Spur and came up the road towards her. His eyes met hers casually as he came level. She was surprised to see a hardness in them that hadn't been there earlier when he helped her with her boat. He obviously hadn't recognised her, and for that she was grateful. Suddenly she felt shame for the way she had landed in such sodden disarray early this morning. No wonder he had scorned her mishandling of the dinghy. She took in a deep breath of salty air, half-wanting to warn him that he wasn't welcome at Harbour Spur.

But suppose he wasn't this Adam Hardwicke after all? Mrs Luke had said the man she had seen would be back when he'd collected his baggage. His baggage – this beautiful yacht? Stephanie moved out of his path and watched him stride away from her up the road, away from the harbour. The magnetic power of the man was disturbing. At once there was a strange emptiness in the bright morning. Maybe she should be spoiling for a fight like Millie, but somehow seeing him like this had taken all the will to do so out of her.

Once back indoors it was hard to concentrate on putting away her shopping. If he really was Adam Hardwicke what could he possibly want with accommodation at Harbour Spur when he had that beautiful yacht that was no doubt fitted out below decks in opulent comfort?

When at last he appeared, she was upstairs on the second floor dusting one of the bedrooms and Millie was downstairs ready for him. At the peremptory knock on the door Stephanie came out of the room and paused at the top of the stairs, her heart thudding. Then she moved down to the first landing and stood with her back to her grandmother's portrait, ready to give support to her aunt if needed.

He stepped inside, uninvited, his dark head towering above her aunt's.

'Good morning, ma'am. I'm here to talk to you about my booking.'

Her aunt's voice was firm as she explained that in the circumstances the room was no longer available.

'What circumstances?' he demanded.

Millie took a deep breath.

'What are you doing here in Polmerrick?' she asked, to Stephanie's amazement.

'Do you interrogate all your guests like this? I think you should explain, ma'am.'

'You can stay somewhere else, that's all.'

'But not at Harbour Spur?'

'It's the one place in Polmerrick you can't get your hands on, and I'll see that you never do.'

He stared down at her without speaking. Disconcerted, Millie glared back at him.

'Don't tell me this isn't your only reason for being here in Polmerrick.'

He seemed to draw himself up to an even greater height.

'The booking was made days ago and I see no good reason why it shouldn't be honoured.'

At once the tone of her aunt's voice rose higher.

'We want none of your sort here, young man.'

He looked at her with a grimness that sent shudders through Stephanie.

'I'm not used to this sort of treatment.' His eyes narrowed as he spoke. 'A minor form of injustice this time, but even so.'

Suddenly he looked up and Stephanie froze. He didn't seem to see her, but gazed steadily at the illuminated portrait of Tamar Trevarrick whose calm face stared back silently. There was a vulnerability in him for a moment that made Stephanie wonder, incredulously, if his reason for being in Polmerrick was other than a mere business project. Millie picked up her small watering can and brandished it at him.

'Out, or I'll have the police on to you. I'll have none of you lot thinking you can have Polmerrick for the taking.'

He moved his intense gaze from the portrait back to Millie. Stephanie made a move forward. He looked up again, this time straight at her. She stopped involuntarily. There was a definite glint of contempt in his eyes now.

'As it happens, I came merely to cancel the accommodation and to pay for it in full. Obviously that won't be necessary. And, oh, boy, you are going to have to whistle for it if you think otherwise!'

Speechless, Millie stared at his retreating back. Then her anger subsided like a deflated balloon and she turned a startled face to Stephanie.

'Oh, Steph, what have I done?'

Stephanie caught hold of her and gave her a quick hug.

'Oh, Millie, I've never seen anything like it. You were great, terrifying.'

Millie smiled briefly.

'We're well rid of the likes of him.'

'Of course we are, Millie.'

'What would I do without you, girl? You're a big support.'

Stephanie smiled at the unexpected praise, but she still felt strangely shaken. Millie replaced the watering can in its place on the shelf.

'So that's that. Now, there's work to be done.'

Stephanie made a move towards the kitchen door, but then she saw the packet. It sat near the telephone, brown against the cream cloth on the table. She snatched it up.

'He left this. I'll go after him!'

'No, Stephanie, wait!'

She took no notice. With her aunt's voice calling after her in protest she opened the door, and ran lightly down the steps.

CHAPTER THREE

Stephanie rushed breathlessly down the slipway behind the tall figure of Adam Hardwicke. He strode along, looking neither left
nor right. She thought she would never catch
him.

'Wait, please, wait!'

There were only moments to spare before
he leaped aboard *Sea Sharon* to follow the
last of the fishing vessels out of the harbour.
Her breath rose painfully in her throat as he
paused and turned round.

'Please!' she managed to gasp out.

She thought she saw a glimmer of friendly
recognition in his eyes that surely had nothing to do with the recent encounter at Harbour Spur. Was it possible that he hadn't
seen her as she stood on the landing
beneath her grandmother's portrait? His

easy charm was apparent now in his warm smile and the way his blue eyes shone in his tanned face.

'Ah, we meet again! Now fully recovered, I see. You must forgive me. You look so different without a boat!'

She glanced briefly down at her neat green skirt, and smiled in spite of herself. A spark of lively interest flickered across his face.

'Are you planning to sail again soon? You'll know about tides of course, but do be careful.'

His assumption that she needed his advice left her speechless. He glanced at the narrow harbour entrance, and made as if to move.

'Unfortunately I've only a few moments.'

She held out the packet.

'This arrived for you at Harbour Spur this morning. You are Mr Adam Hardwicke?'

There was peculiar pleasure in saying his name out loud.

'Harbour Spur?'

The hardness was back in his voice now.

Ignoring the parcel, he looked at her closely.

'So they allow you time off, do they?'

'You are Mr Adam Hardwicke?'

He nodded. Her quick intake of breath was as much to steady her own senses as to remind herself of why she was here. She stood straight, and looked back at him unsmilingly with the packet in her hand.

'You came to Harbour Spur, and you made threats.'

'That is between the proprietor and myself.'

Stephanie's eyes blazed.

'We're all devastated by the ugly rumours flying about the place. Can you wonder you're not welcome?'

He turned his head slightly and gazed at the quiet harbour. A lone seagull swept low over the water, letting out an eerie call. Only *Sea Sharon* was berthed now. The quay on the other side seemed ominously deserted.

'We have to know what's going on, and who's behind it all. My aunt...'

'Your aunt?'

'You came threatening her as if you had a perfect right to enter Harbour Spur.'

'Harbour Spur is your home?'

'Of course it's my home. I live there.'

He looked disconcerted.

'Then you're not merely an employee? Your aunt is the owner of Harbour Spur?'

'That's what I said.'

His eyes narrowed.

'A termagant, yes, siree!'

Stephanie took a deep breath.

'We need to know what's going to happen to Polmerrick. Suddenly we hear there's to be a take-over, then you appear. It's tempting to put two and two together.'

'And make five? So that's what that aunt of yours did?'

'You mean there's no truth in it? No connection?'

The expression in his eyes told her nothing.

'I've got to go or it'll be too late to get out on this tide. I'll be back, you can be certain of that. And when I do I need to talk. I mean to own Harbour Spur, given time.'

'No way!' she cried.

The yacht was lower in the water now and pulling away from the quay as if anxious to be gone. He paused only to throw back over his shoulder, 'If Polmerrick is left alone it's finished. I'll be back!'

A moment later the engine sprang to life. Stephanie was still standing, dazed, as *Sea Sharon* nosed her way out of the harbour. Then she, too, came to life and sprang up the slipway to get a better view of the yacht's direction. She ran back the way she had come, but instead of going into the house she ran up the cliff path and stood at the top gazing out to sea.

Sea Sharon looked small on the wide expanse, growing ever smaller with each moment. At last Stephanie could see her no more. Her sense of loss was acute, even though the man was her enemy. He said he wanted Harbour Spur and meant to have it! But why? If he was behind the purchase of the village the ownership of one cottage was neither here nor there. It simply didn't make sense.

She walked back down the cliff to Harbour Spur. Only a short time had passed since she had run out of the house with the intention of giving him the packet and getting to the bottom of his threats. She had done neither. Instead she felt a strange unease.

To her surprise her aunt was coming out of the front door with her watering can in her hand. Hastily Stephanie thrust the packet out of sight in the pocket of her skirt.

'The baskets need a lot of seeing to in this weather,' Millie said as she saw Stephanie.

Only the glint in her eyes gave away her real reason for her not staying indoors. She weaved the watering can, and drops flew out.

'So, what did he say?'

Stephanie was unable to dismiss the disturbing picture of the man from her mind.

'It's important I see the Rosslyons,' she said. 'There's something I need to verify.'

'So he did say something?'

Stephanie shook her head. Every inch of Adam Hardwicke's powerful body indicated that no-one got the better of him. She was sure that only the necessity of his taking *Sea Sharon* out on the tide now had prevented him from further attack immediately. There was no doubt that he would be back, for Harbour Spur, he had threatened, unbelievable as it sounded.

'So you're no nearer finding out the truth?' Millie asked.

Stephanie shook her head. There had been something odd in the way he had gazed on the portrait of her grandmother that made her think that his intention to get inside their home was strong. Millie emptied the watering can, not caring that the water surged out of the basket on to the ground beneath.

'We'd better get going on our fight to save Polmerrick.'

'Don't do anything about it until I get back from Rosslyon House, Millie. It's important. Let's get the facts straight first and then we'll know what we're about. Promise?'

Her aunt sighed.

'All right, Steph, I promise. But only till you get back.'

Millie would keep her word once she had given it. No need to tell her yet about Harbour Spur being important to this stranger for some unaccountable reason. Millie was incensed enough as it was.

As she set about their lunch preparations Stephanie was unable to banish the thought of Adam Hardwicke from her thoughts. Her mind would keep dwelling on the way he had looked through her as she stood beneath the portrait. What would Tamar Trevarrick have made of a complete stranger demanding to have their home just like that? She tossed the question round in her mind without finding any sensible answer.

It was only just after two o'clock when Stephanie hurried up the drive to Rosslyon House, the rising wind teasing her hair. She brushed it out of her eyes, reminded of the unexpected gust that had caused her such humiliation as she landed at his feet on the beach this morning. She would not think of Adam Hardwicke, yet how could she help it when her reason for coming to Rosslyon House this afternoon was because of him?

She had often come this way in the old days when she and Nick had been seeing a lot of each other. It still hurt, just a little, that he had not contacted her at all since the Christmas Ball when he had made the surprising announcement of his engagement to someone else. On first sight the huge hall looked just the same, but as she followed the girl who had opened the door Stephanie saw that several family portraits were no longer on the walls.

There was a delicate smell of pot-pourri about the sitting-room. Stephanie had expected to see her elderly friend seated in her usual chair, but the room was empty. She moved to the French windows and stood looking out at the wide expanse of lawn, hoping that Mrs Rosslyon was well enough to see her. There was a movement behind her, and she looked round. Her mouth dropped open. There stood Nick!

He looked just the same. His pure white shirt bulged only a little more over his dark trousers. His rosy, good-tempered face beamed at her as if sure of her pleasure in seeing him.

'Steph, it's great to see you.'

She took a deep breath.

'But I thought…'

He moved towards her and caught hold of both her hands, pressing them in his own warm ones for a moment.

'Mother said you were coming.'

She smiled. A vision of Adam's determined stance in the hall of her home shot, unbidden, into her mind.

'It's about the village, Nick.'

He gestured her towards the sofa.

'We'd never have made a go of it. Miranda and me.'

Stephanie looked at him in astonishment as she sat down.

'You mean…'

'The engagement's off. I thought you knew, Steph.'

'And you think that's why I came?'

She stared at him, horrified, and saw that he was smiling.

'How could I know, or even be interested?'

'Mother thinks it would never have worked,' he said as if he hadn't heard her. 'No, I'm well out of it.'

He seated himself on the sofa next to her. Stephanie could find nothing to say for a moment. He looked genuinely pleased to be with her again. His engagement might never have happened.

'Mother always had a soft spot for you, Steph.'

'About the village, Nick,' she insisted before he had time to frame the words she saw hovering on his lips. 'I must know what's going on.'

He smiled, and his eyes seemed to disappear.

'You heard then?'

Her lifeblood seemed to drain from her body. Until now there had been a glimmer of hope, weak, of course, and almost obliterated by all that had happened since her return to Polmerrick, but hope all the same. Now it was dashed.

'You're to sell Polmerrick?'

Her voice was weak. Nick looked at her in alarm.

'You don't mind, do you, Steph? Harbour Spur belongs to your family. I made it clear it wasn't included in the sale.'

'How could you think of selling the village, Nick? It's bound to change everything if someone else gets hold of it and rips it apart. Who will care for Polmerrick as your family has for years and years?'

'What would you do, Steph, let it all go to rack and ruin?'

'But it doesn't have to. There's money to be made from boats using the facilities if they are modernised just a bit without spoiling everything. Don't you even care?'

Nick didn't answer for a moment. He

gazed into space as if he was miles away. Then he turned towards her, and his smile deepened.

'Now that Miranda's pulled out ... well, no, frankly, I don't care. There's no incentive for me to work from here anymore. I need to be up country not down here in this god-forsaken place. Far more sensible to move out and let someone else take over the house and the whole village to develop. It's sound, economic sense.'

For a second Stephanie couldn't speak. Then a burst of rage rose in her to such a pitch that she felt like striking out at his bland, uncaring face.

'You'd leave your family home, your roots? You'd move your mother? You'd leave Polmerrick in the hands of developers and not care what happens to the place?'

He smiled again, but his eyes looked troubled now as he smoothed his fine hair away from his forehead. Even at this moment Stephanie couldn't help comparing it with Adam Hardwicke's abundant dark mop. A vision of Adam's compelling strength shot into her mind and made her gasp.

'Hey, steady on!' he said rather uncomfortably.

'You did all this behind our backs. Why didn't you tell people what was going on?'

'What good would that have done? The proposed marina is an excellent idea. Large enough for bigger vessels to use, a high-class restaurant close to the moorings, bars, possibly amusements for the kids while their parents are indulging themselves. It can only be good for business for you, Steph. Harbour Spur is in a prime position.'

'What for? Accommodation for the rich crowd? They won't want Harbour Spur. And our old clients won't come to overlook all that hullabaloo. We'll be forced to close down.'

'Your aunt must have made a pretty penny through the years. She could move out, find some small place that suits her.'

Stephanie clenched her hands. Unable to trust herself to speak, she turned away, struggling for control. She heard him move towards the window, and at last turned to look at him. He stood with his back to her with his hands in his trouser pockets.

'I told you, Steph, things change. I've had an offer, you see, a good one, and I've accepted it. It's in the hands of the solicitors.'

'But how did they get planning permission so soon? I can't believe how it was done.'

'Planning permission? He wants to go ahead without planning permission.'

'But he can't!'

'I mean he'll apply for it afterwards. He seems confident he'll get it.'

'Oh, please, Nick, think again.'

'The man's offering a good price. No way will we get that from elsewhere without outline planning permission.'

'Oh, Nick!'

His eyes clouded a moment, and then were clear again. In them she saw a dawning of purpose. He moved towards her, smiling.

'We always were suited, weren't we, right

from the earliest days? Sit down again, Steph.'

He perched himself on the edge of the desk, and sat leaning slightly towards her as she plumped down on the sofa again. A sort of bland confidence oozed out of him that was hard to penetrate. She knew that Nick had always looked after Nick. So why was she expecting him to change suddenly? His smile deepened, and she saw tiny lines at the sides of his wide mouth she hadn't seen before. She moved back a little from him, but he didn't seem to notice.

'Anyway, the development will be good for the place, Steph. Bring new life to Polmerrick, not to mention more employment. The place has been dead for years, and it's bound to get worse.'

He drummed his fingers on one hand on the desk. He turned back to her, and she could see he was serious.

'There will never be another offer like this, Steph. The Canadian's determined to have the place. That's exactly what will happen, unless…'

'Unless what?' she cried.

'Unless, Steph, you agree to be more than friends.'

'What are you saying?'

He moved closer to her.

'I think you know what I mean, Steph.'

Stunned, she stared back at him. For two seconds there was no sound in the room. He was so earnest that she couldn't laugh it off as the joke she wished it were. Once she had cared for Nick. Because of it she had to reply seriously now, but somehow the words wouldn't come. She felt she would choke.

'Come on, Steph, what do you say? Let's start again at the beginning. Mother'll be pleased. The Canadian can take a running jump. With you at my side, Steph, I'll be the happiest man alive. And if it'll make you happy we'll stay and do what you want about the village.'

Outside, the wind scurried round the house. She said nothing for a long moment.

'Steph, I'm asking you to be my wife. We'll

be partners here. We don't have to go away. We'll stay if you want, Steph. What d'you say? Marry me!'

Released suddenly from her frozen surprise, Stephanie leaped up and retreated towards the door. With her hand on the handle she looked at him wildly.

'I can't, Nick. I can't. It's not possible.'

Naked disappointment shone from his face and the confidence seemed to drain from him. For a moment he was like the Nick she used to know, following her blindly into all sorts of scrapes that meant trouble for them both. She turned and ran. It wasn't until she arrived at Harbour Spur that she realised that her vehemence must have surprised Nick to say the least.

They had always been friends, indeed more than that. If she agreed to his wish to continue where they had left off and then agree to marry him, it would be the answer to all the worries about the take-over of Polmerrick. The take-over would never happen. Nick would pull out from the agreement.

Adam Hardwicke would never get his hands on the village, or pose a threat to Harbour Spur itself.

CHAPTER FOUR

Stepping into the peace of Harbour Spur, Stephanie paused for a moment. From the deep silence in the house, Millie must be busy elsewhere. Stealthily she crept up the stairs, as usual glancing up at her grandmother's portrait on the wall halfway up. The fitful sunshine hadn't quite reached the hall window and the portrait was in shadow.

Stephanie didn't need to see clearly to know exactly how her grandmother looked as she leaned on the harbour wall with the blue sea behind her. What would Tamar Trevarrick have done in these circumstances? There was no answer for Stephanie in the calm grey eyes of the young girl looking down at her. This was her own problem, and she had to deal with it in her own way – and that, at the moment, was a need to get away somewhere on her own to think things through before facing her aunt.

Stephanie was out of her skirt and blouse and into shorts and T-shirt in moments. Grabbing cagoule and lifejacket she slipped downstairs again, collected the sail bag and went out into the fresh, salty air. On the beach the outgoing tide had left a rim of brown seaweed. Nick Rosslyon's astonishing words still pounded inside her head.

Once on the water, though, the wind on her face helped dispel them. If only she had time to spend the day with Dinah at Trebithick. Her friend's breezy commonsense was what she needed at the moment. On impulse she decided to make for the tiny cove where they used to go for picnics years ago. She would be alone there, out of sight for a short, precious time, to help her come to terms with all that had happened.

The beach shelved steeply and with the wind behind her Stephanie had an easy landing. Not even bothering to unzip her lifejacket, she sat on the sand with her hands round her knees thinking of Polmerrick. Millie certainly wouldn't force her into an unhappy marriage even if she knew what Nick wanted. And who was to say that Nick Rosslyon would keep his word once the wedding ring was on her finger?

Stephanie raised her eyes and looked out to sea, stiffening as she saw a yacht, white-sailed, making for Polmerrick. *Sea Sharon?* For a few moments she watched, glad that she had come to shore, out of sight. But the peace was ruined for her now. When at last the white sails were out of sight she launched her boat and headed out at an angle until she was well clear of the cliffs. Not a sign of anything, thank goodness. *Sea Sharon* was safely in harbour.

Back at Harbour Spur, Mrs Luke had already told Millie about Nick's broken engagement. As Stephanie went in, Millie, her face flushed, started in on Nick Rosslyon at once. She paused for breath only when Stephanie sat down at the table and put her head in her hands.

'You've taken this badly, Steph. Don't tell me you care for that good-for-nothing after all.'

Stephanie raised her head.

'Oh, Millie, of course not.'

'Whom did you see, his mother?'

'I saw Nick himself.'

'Nick? No doubt thinking you'd be pleased, falling into his arms.'

This was too near the truth for comfort.

'Millie, leave it now. It's done, and it makes no difference. His engagement's off, and that's that. And it's true he's selling Polmerrick in its entirety. He seemed to think that not splitting up the village would be good for the place. I don't know. I don't know anything any more.'

'So that man will get everything?'

'Except Harbour Spur.'

'Definitely not Harbour Spur!'

'Millie, if the sale of the village happens, and it's likely to, are you sure you want to stay here? Wouldn't it be better to sell up and move out to something smaller? You could get a good price. Invested wisely it could mean security for you for the rest of your life.'

'Are you mad, girl? It's your home and always will be as far as I'm concerned. It's for you, Steph.'

'You, too, Millie.'

Her aunt looked at her strangely.

'Well, yes,' she said and sprang up to brush invisible crumbs off the table.

'You know there's no planning permission for anything yet?' Stephanie said.

'There will be.'

'I suppose so. It explains why Nick is so keen to get this sale sorted out quickly.'

'Then we must make sure he loses the sale,' Millie declared.

Stephanie smiled, glad that her aunt said no more about the Rosslyons for the moment. It was impossible to forget that she alone had the power to stop all this. If she had agreed to Nick Rosslyon's proposal, Polmerrick would be safe from the developer. There would be none of the worry, the heartbreak, the frustration.

To her dismay, Stephanie discovered next morning that Adam Hardwicke's forgotten packet was still in her pocket. About to load the washing machine, she pulled out the packet, and looked at it. Then, on hearing her aunt come into the kitchen, she slipped it out of sight.

'Mrs Luke will be here in a minute,' Millie said. 'You deserve some more time off, Steph, seeing we've few guests. Why not go for a sail or something?'

'I might just do that if I'm not needed here for a while. I'll sail over to Trebithick to see Dinah if she's at home. Millie, you're an angel.'

'Do you good, Steph. Stay the night if you want.'

'I might just do that. Pity she's not on the phone or I could warn her I'm coming.'

She was soon ready. They might even get a swim and with her bikini on under her shorts and shirt she was ready for anything. Smiling to herself Stephanie let herself out of the front door and ran lightly down the steps with her sailing bag on her shoulder and the packet in her hand. She hoped Millie wasn't watching as she turned away from the harbour wall and headed for the slipway.

To her surprise his yacht wasn't there. Perhaps she had imagined it heading towards the harbour. But no. Her own turbulent feelings were proof of that. Slowly she retraced her steps towards the beach. The tide was going out now and nothing larger than a small dinghy could come in and out of the harbour. There was just a chance that the yacht was tied up to the high wall outside as boats often were. Stephanie ran to the outer wall, the wind catching her in a sudden gust. She was right. Here, out of the shelter of the harbour, *Sea Sharon* rose and fell with the sea.

There was no-one on deck. She hesitated, holding the packet in her hand as if it was full of dynamite. Now was her chance to get rid of it quickly. She looked round at the now deserted quayside, and then leaped on board. As she landed, she felt the deck move away from the quay. Frozen with horror, she saw something she had failed to notice before. No ropes held *Sea Sharon* tied to the bollards. At the same moment, the vessel shuddered as the engine fired.

Adam Hardwicke appeared at once to take the wheel. His surprise as he saw Stephanie was genuine, she was sure of that. There was surprise and a flicker of something else she couldn't quite fathom. Interest, relief? Impossible to tell.

She stared at him in dismay for the few precious seconds it might have been possible to leap back on to the outer wall. With one hand guiding the wheel, he smiled, his bright eyes lighting up his face.

'So, I have a stowaway? Excellent. Welcome aboard!'

She waved the packet at him, her mouth dry.

'I've got to get off. I forgot to give you this.'

His laugh now had a confident ring to it.

'Too late. I've only just made it in the falling tide. No way can I get back even to the outer wall now.'

She knew this only too well. She had missed her opportunity.

'You saw me,' she cried. 'You did this deliberately!'

It was a ridiculous accusation, of course. How could he have seen her!

'So I can see through hulls can I? News to me.'

Already they were passing the arm of the harbour wall. She looked frantically at Harbour Spur standing square and solid, facing the sea. It was fading into the background more with every second that passed. She turned to face him, shaking. He stood unperturbed at the wheel, a small smile at the corners of his mouth as they met the choppier water of the open sea. He might have been taking her for a joy ride round the bay for all the reaction her appearance on the deck of *Sea Sharon* had on him. Suddenly the engine died. Only the slapping of the waves on the hull disturbed the air.

'Take the wheel,' he ordered, with a movement of his dark head.

He leaped down below, as Stephanie sprang to hold on to the wheel. The engine gave a splutter, flickered again, and then died, and all the time the ebb tide was taking the yacht with it. For the time it took Adam to move forward to begin hoisting sail she stood motionless with her hands holding hard to the wheel. Then, gradually, she moved it round so that they began to bear round in a wide arc. A wave, catching the bow, broke over Adam in swirling spray.

He reacted with a shout of indignation. For a heart-stopping second he stood outlined against the sea. Then he moved back towards her. She stiffened herself for the blazing anger she knew would come. With water pouring from him he took the wheel from her and headed the yacht round again and out to sea. Hardly daring to look at him, she backed as far away as she could as he bent to pick up the packet she had dropped on the deck.

'Take that,' he said, throwing it at her. 'Take care of it this time. Put it down in the galley, and report back here.'

She was in no position to argue. Clutching anything she could get hold of to steady herself against the rolling of the boat, she did as she was told. Down below the movement seemed worse. Where was he taking her? Not back to shore, that was certain, but how far out to sea did he intend to go? Her mouth was dry as she placed the packet on the shelf above the tiny sink and then stumbled back on deck.

She was astounded to see that Adam was smiling. This was worse than anger, much worse. What had he in mind now? She looked at him suspiciously as he stood relaxed at the wheel, apparently unconscious of any discomfort. His white T-shirt clung to his body like wet plastic and water dripped down his tanned face in rivulets.

Even though he hadn't hoisted any more sail they were moving fast. At any other time Stephanie would have delighted in their speed. Never had she sailed this far out in her own dinghy. It was exhilarating.

'Take the wheel,' he ordered. 'Keep her on course this time while I attend to the engine.'

'On course for where?' she cried. 'Where are we going?'

'Take it,' he said again, his voice hard.

As she took the wheel from him his hand brushed hers with a gesture she found disturbing. Polmerrick and dry land was a thin line behind them now, and the wind was gusting. She dare not try anything on in these conditions, inexperienced as she was with anything of *Sea Sharon's* size. She listened for the welcome sound of engine noise, but there was nothing, only the roar of the wind in the sail and the water slapping high on the prow.

Sea Sharon was hard to hold in the rising wind. Every now and again Stephanie's shoulders felt wrenched out of their sockets as she struggled to hold the yacht on course in the strong gusts that set it shuddering. Adam was a long time down below. When at last he emerged, rubbing his hands on a piece of cloth, she saw that he had changed into dry clothes and was now wearing a navy sweatshirt and white shorts. On deck he pulled on yellow oilskins.

Suddenly, Stephanie, aware that she was cold, shivered.

'I want to go back, now.'

'So you're not enjoying this?'

It was obvious that he was from the glint in his eyes and the small smile quirking the corners of his mouth. He took the wheel from her, and with a nod of his dark head indicated that she was free to move away.

'Get something warmer on. You'll feel better.'

'Better?' she flashed back at him as she found her sail bag where she had dropped it.

She opened it with shaking hands and pulled out her jersey and cagoule.

'No way will I feel better. I want to go back in nearer the shore.'

He wouldn't take any notice of her request, she knew, but she felt the need to protest.

'You've no right to take me with you,' she said, shivering.

'Get your life jacket on, too,' he ordered. 'The wind's getting up. Do as I say.'

'So where's yours?' she retorted as she zipped up her cagoule.

His brow darkened.

'All in good time. Just do as I say.'

'Tell me where we're going,' she demanded. 'If you know, that is. We're halfway across the bay already. Take me back.'

He smiled.

'No way. Stowaways take the consequences of their actions. I didn't ask you to come aboard though I'm delighted you did. I can use some help and you seem capable enough.'

'Enough for what? We'll be round the headland in a minute. Where are we going?'

'No going back now. I'm due at Falmouth to meet my crew there with the dinghy. The engine needs work done on it, too, and it will be done there. No problem. Now be a good girl, and stop complaining. After all, you're getting a free trip. Don't you owe me something for that?'

He grinned at her again, and she opened her mouth to retort that she wanted no such thing. Before she could frame the words there was a crash as a gigantic wave thundered aboard.

'We're in for worse if I'm not mistaken.'

His voice was serious now, with a touch of determination that made her wince. Was he taking them far out from land to ride out the storm away from the rocky coastline? She couldn't tell how far they had come, but it seemed likely. In that case there was the sail to be lowered. But he made no attempt to hand over the wheel again so that he could move forward to release the sheets and pull it down. So, he intended to sail on carrying the amount of sail they had set out with.

She gripped the handrail with icy hands, silently willing him to go about and bring *Sea Sharon* closer in to shore. He seemed to be revelling in the speed, and the roaring of the wind and the crashing of the great seas that rolled on to the heaving deck. It got worse as the moment passed.

'We'll go about,' he shouted at last.

She knew she had to take the helm while he crawled forward to do what had to be done with the sail. In this roaring noise, would she hear his order to pull the wheel round at the right moment so that *Sea Sharon* would change direction?

His lifejacket was on now, and to her relief he attached the safety line to the rail. What she would do if he fell overboard she dare not think.

'Can you hold her?' he shouted. 'Wait for my signal and pull her round.'

She bit her lips hard in concentration as she hung desperately to the wheel, at the same time watching Adam move forward to the mast. For a moment he was hidden, and then she saw him again. At his signal she slewed the wheel round, and then let out a huge, relieved gasp as she saw the sail come down. He crawled back towards her, un-hooked himself and took the wheel from her with hands that were strong and firm.

The wind was still fierce and the waves high. *Sea Sharon* was running before it now. There was satisfaction in knowing that they were moving back towards land even though at a wide angle that was taking them miles away down the coast from Polmerrick. Even so there was no relaxing for the helmsman. He stood braced against the wheel, staring straight ahead. Stephanie held tight to the handrail, and even when the rain came, lashing them with a fury she wouldn't have thought possible, she remained where she was.

She had never sailed before in anything the size of this. In her own small dinghy she was in command, and able to make her own decisions. Now, though, her very life depended on the way this man handled *Sea Sharon*. She wanted to stay on deck at his side. They must have sailed many sea miles by the time he acknowledged her presence again.

'Get below,' he said tersely. 'The rain will soak you.'

'Have you only just noticed the rain? I'm staying here until we reach harbour.'

'Then you'll be here a long time. I shan't make for Falmouth tonight after all. No sense when it's as bad as this.'

'So where to?'

He shrugged, still staring ahead.

'We're in for a good, long blow. All night probably.'

Stephanie bit her lip. She had no idea where they were. The distant headlands were unrecognisable in the gloom of the darkened sky. All the time, though, she knew they were getting closer to land even though Adam moved the helm around slightly so that *Sea Sharon* veered away a fraction. Suddenly there was an almighty crash, and she thought they were over. She was flung hard against the rail as the boat shuddered and then ploughed on through the heaving sea.

'All right?' Adam shouted.

He didn't look at her to check but kept his gaze fixed ahead.

'I'm OK,' she gasped, clutching her right

arm and silently willing the pain in it to disappear.

Adam had ordered her below, but she had stayed. It was her own fault if she was hurt. He allowed himself a quick glance in her direction, and his mouth tightened. It was almost as if he guessed that she was lying. She looked around, and saw that the distant cliffs were not as high as before. An indent in them had appeared through the murk. The rain was stopping now, but the wind still gusted and the waves were high.

Slowly Adam eased the wheel round again. He threw her a speculative glance.

'I think we can make it.'

'Through there? It's not possible.'

'If we don't want to stay out here all night we'll have to try our luck in that estuary.'

'If you're sure,' she shouted back through the continuous noise of wind and sea.

'You know the risks. Are you game?'

She tried to smile, but her face felt cold and drawn.

'Of course. I told you, I'm all right.'

'Good girl.'

She was surprised at the warmth that flooded through her at his words. They were moving fast towards shore now. Beside her Adam stood straight, a grim expression on his face. Then *Sea Sharon* made for the opening that seemed to come at them with alarming speed.

CHAPTER FIVE

Stephanie gazed at the two arms of the inlet, praying that no submerged rocks guarded the entrance. Once inside, the roaring wind died a little. With the lessening of speed the motion of the waves got to her, and for the first time she felt queasy. She took a deep breath. Beside her Adam grunted in satisfaction as he pulled the wheel round so that the yacht was head to wind.

At once he went forward to lower the anchor and the sudden cessation of movement made Stephanie gulp. It took all her willpower to control her surge of sickness.

'Success,' he shouted back. 'We'll be OK in here, yes, siree. With luck the storm will be gone by morning.'

He came back towards her, and as she raised her face towards him she surprised an expression of deep concern on his own. She blinked back weak tears and he caught hold of her shoulder.

'You all right?'

She winced, and tried to stand upright but the effort was too much for her. All at once she slumped down, and the next thing she knew she was lying on the deck, supported by Adam's strong arm.

'You need food and a rest,' he said. 'You were great, a steady nerve, and courage.'

Warmth filled her at his praise.

'Let me take a look at that arm.'

She raised herself on her elbow.

'If you could help me get my lifejacket off.'

He was up at once, removing his own, and peeling off his wet oilskins before helping her. At once she felt better even though she ached all over. She rolled up the sleeve of her sweatshirt to reveal bruising that was already turning a deep brownish purple. Adam whistled between his teeth as he looked at it. Then he probed her arm with gentle fingers.

'You gave that quite a bash, but I don't

think there are any bones broken.'

He sounded so concerned that she felt tears spring to her eyes again. Hastily, she wiped them away. It was only now that they were safe that she realised that it was Adam's strength and expertise that had got them safely to this place. She watched him as he did what had to be done with the sails and sheets.

'Where did you learn to sail like that?' she asked at last.

'Here and there. My family likes sailing. I learned in the roughest of conditions. I was my grandfather's regular crew.'

He smiled, but then frowned as if reminded of something painful.

'Food,' he said at last.

Eating was the last thing she had on her mind, but when he produced hot soup to give comforting warmth and plenty of bread she found she was unexpectedly hungry.

'Better?' he asked as they finished eating and he got up to make tea.

Stephanie smiled, warm and comfortable

for the first time for hours. She glanced at her watch and saw it was eight o'clock. She wished she had more energy, but all she could do was sit slumped on the seat. Already her eyelids were drooping. The rocking of the boat at anchor was soothing.

Stephanie slept well that night, far better than she would have thought possible when she crawled into the borrowed sleeping bag in the berth in the main cabin that Adam, yawning, had allocated to her. By this time his face looked drawn and pale, and his dark hair clung damply to his head. Their gruelling sail was enough to exhaust anyone, even a man of such strength and vigour.

Waking early, she stretched out luxuriously. There were no sounds yet of Adam moving about in the forward cabin. The silence now was enchanting. She lay still for a moment, savouring the knowledge that Adam was only a few feet or so away. For the first time in her life she felt the naturalness of being near a man whose charm made her forget everything else. She wanted to be with him.

Nothing else seemed important as she lay there on the gently-moving boat that yesterday had seemed like a prison.

At last, cautiously, she sat up. Her movement was enough to stir the magic a little so that reality began to creep in. She couldn't remain here, becalmed for ever. A calm start to the day was all right if enough wind got up later to ensure a choice of how long they remained here. Slipping out of her bunk, she peered through the porthole. A small, sandy beach enclosed by rocky cliffs was close by. The water between was invitingly smooth, and beneath her T-shirt she wore her bikini.

Suddenly she needed to feel the freshness of cold water on her skin. Moments later she was clambering up on deck. Already the sun was above the low cliffs. She might have been the only person alive on this lovely morning as she slipped quietly overboard. Although the water was icy it was exhilarating. Careful not to splash, she swam in a wide circle round the boat, and then made for the shore, breathing deeply as she waded the last few feet on to the sand. Farther up where it was dry and warm she sat down with her hands clasped round her legs and the sunshine warm on her back.

Sea Sharon moved slightly at anchor, and little ripples teased the edge of the sand. There was movement on the yacht's deck as Adam appeared wearing black bathing trunks, a white towel slung round his neck. She watched him throw the towel down and stand poised to dive overboard. There wasn't an ounce of excess fat on his magnificently proportioned body.

He dived in, and then swam strongly away, his dark head moving swiftly through the water. Then he turned to swim back. Seconds later, he was wading ashore, shaking the moisture from his hair. His powerful shoulders glistened as the sun caught them, and water trickled in rivulets down his broad chest and muscular thighs.

Stephanie couldn't quite control the lift of her heart as he came towards her across the silver sand. It was intoxicating, the sun and the warm air and the sight of the tall, dark-haired man outlined against the sea.

'Hi, there,' he greeted her. 'You had the right idea. Sleep well?'

Stephanie jumped to her feet.

'Surprisingly well. And you?'

'Like a log. I'm off to see what's round the corner. Coming?'

He didn't wait for her reply but strode off towards the rocks at one side of the cove. They were sharp with limpet shells, and pressed into her bare feet as she followed him. He went quickly, not looking back. They came to hard, wet sand at the base of taller cliffs where isolated needles of rock towered into the sky.

'It's another world,' she breathed. 'Beautiful!'

'Beautiful indeed.'

He flung back his head to gaze at the pinnacles.

'Boy, are they incredible! How many millions of years have gone into the making of these?'

She could hardly bear the force of longing that filled her as she looked at him. She turned away, kneeling to peer into a rock pool where myriads of tiny fish scurried and pretending an interest in them. What was it about this man that had penetrated her defences so unexpectedly?

She felt him move towards her. Scrambling to her feet, she flicked back her hair from her face. His arm was round her in an instant pulling her urgently away from the edge of the pool. A pulse throbbed in his throat.

'Stephanie,' he said in a voice deep, vibrant.

She stood quite still, unable to breathe, and then gave a sigh as his lips found hers. Some deep feeling darted deep within her, sharp, piercing, sweet, a half-forgotten reaction to the nearness of a man. She felt carried away on a wave of excitement.

'You no longer fight me,' he whispered.

'Adam, oh, Adam!'

She had never felt like this before. His eyes

glowed as he looked at her. Her own, she felt sure, gave back an answering warmth.

'My love.'

His words, soft as the breeze, caressed her. She gave a low moan as his lips pressed down hard on hers once more. When he moved away from her again she felt a quick sharp sense of loss.

'Your arm,' he murmured. 'Is it painful still?'

She had almost forgotten about it. Now he took it in his hands and looked at it as if he could see right through to the bone. It was a concerned, friendly gesture.

'It's as well the bruise came out like this,' he said, letting his hands drop. 'I wouldn't have hurt you for the world. You know that, Stephanie?'

His smile was warm, and his eyes a brilliant blue.

'And that's not only because you were a splendid crew in yesterday's storm.'

She felt a soft glow in her cheeks. His praise was even sweeter this morning now that she knew that he was beginning to mean a great deal more to her than Nick Rosslyon had ever done. At the thought of Nick her face clouded and she moved away slightly. They began to walk back the way they had come. Adam seemed to sense at once that some shadow had clouded the moment.

'Let's sit down for a while,' he said.

He gazed at her with an expression of such sweetness that her heart seemed to swell within her.

'There's something I have to say to you.'

She sat next to him, smiling and relaxed. What could he say that would add more pleasure to this perfect time? She saw an answering gleam in his own gaze that delighted her. The sunlight caressed her skin. She was aware of the gentle lap of the water and the soft crying of some sea bird far away. He leaned towards her, looking serious.

'I'm committed to something important, Stephanie. I need to tell you, so that you understand how it is with me.'

His voice deepened. She raised her chin, feeling again a faint echo of the excitement and anticipation that had lifted her a moment ago.

'I have something to show you, too, the contents of the packet. It's a love letter written by someone long ago.'

'A love letter?' she said in puzzled surprise.

'You need to see it, Stephanie, to understand. Because of it, there is something I have to do.'

She sat quite still, watching him as he stared across the inlet away from the beach. He looked troubled now, and vulnerable and she could hardly bear it. She put out her hand to stroke his arm. He put his own warm one over it, and pressed hers. In that simple gesture was all the feeling in the world. She smiled, content.

'There's a lot to be said, Stephanie, a lot to explain.'

'It can wait a little longer if you like, Adam. Wait until you show me the letter, and then tell me all at once.'

He pressed her hand again, and let it go, smiling suddenly.

'You're right, my love. I don't know about you but that swim has made me ravenous.'

'Me, too,' she replied, smiling also.

He let her swim ahead of him and climb aboard first. He shook himself and then reached for the towel.

'Here, Stephanie, have this. You're shivering.'

She took it from him gratefully, and buried her face in it for a moment before wrapping it round her shoulders.

'Wait here,' he ordered. 'I'll go below and dig out something warm for you to put on.'

'I'll soon dry out,' she called after him. 'The sun's hot already. I'll be all right.'

But he had gone. She stood by the rail, rubbing the towel gently across her shoulders. All her aches and pains of last evening had vanished. Only the bruise on her arm hurt just a little. It seemed to her that she could still feel Adam's surprisingly gentle touch on her skin as he examined it. She marvelled that this man whom she had loathed for what he planned to do to Polmerrick now held her heart in the hollow of his hand.

In a few moments he was back on deck, wearing shorts and T-shirt. The red sweatshirt he held out to her was immense and almost covered her completely as she pulled it on over her wet bikini. They were both hungry, and made short work of the cereal, fruit and toast Adam produced.

They had washed up the breakfast things in the small galley and were back in the main cabin before Stephanie raised the subject of their return to Polmerrick. Following her up the steps to the deck, Adam threw back his head and gazed at the cloudless sky.

'We need wind to get us into Falmouth under sail. My two crew members are there with the dinghy, and the engine needs a big repair job. So, we stay here for the moment. There's no other way.'

His expression belied the faint regret in his voice. She felt regret, too, in spite of good sense beginning to assert itself. He licked his finger and then held it up in the air to test the wind direction.

'A faint stir,' he said. 'We may be lucky yet. I've a feeling we will be.'

She nodded, and glanced briefly at the sandy beach of the cove, wondering how Adam would broach the subject he wished to talk about now that they were back on board. He seemed to read her thoughts.

'What do you say, work first and then talk? Or do you want to talk first?'

'You decide.'

'The rigging will have to be checked after the bashing it got yesterday. Care to give a hand?'

She would have enjoyed it if there had been more sign that wind was coming up. When the checking was done to Adam's satisfaction he disappeared into the galley and came back with two mugs of coffee. The sun was really warm now, too hot for the thick sweatshirt. In her own shorts and T-shirt once more Stephanie felt comfortable as they sat on deck to drink. Adam had brought the open packet up with him, and drew out the contents.

'There's a letter from my lawyer,' he said. 'With it he encloses a copy of a document I needed. Care to see it?'

She placed her half-empty mug down at her feet as she took the paper from him and sat with bent head attempting to make sense of it. At last she raised her face.

'I don't understand. Why did you want me to see this?'

'It's a love letter, written by my grandfather when he was a young man and it's been carefully preserved. You can see it's a happy letter delighting in his Tazie's love for him and telling her of his relief that they had a house to share.'

His voice was deep with emotion.

'But I don't quite see what it's all about,' she said.

'An injustice was done to him. It rankled

for the rest of his life.'

He gazed at the sea beyond the headland and she could see in his face a determination that hardened his features to granite.

'I still don't understand, Adam.'

'She meant so much to him, you see, the recipient of the letter, his Tazie. He never forgot her.'

He refolded the letter, replaced it with the others in the envelope and put it down at his side. Then he seemed to relax a little.

'As a young boy in Toronto, I grew up on the stories James used to tell.'

'Your grandfather?'

He nodded.

'He painted little pictures of her for me, on scraps of tree bark and on the smooth pebbles we found at the lakeside.'

He stopped speaking suddenly and leaned forward and took her own face in his hands. She knew it wasn't herself he was seeing, but this long-ago girl his grandfather, James, had loved so much.

'But what happened?' she whispered as he

let his hands drop. 'What was the injustice that was done to him?'

'He came to this country as a young man. It was here they met and fell in love. But they had to part. Yet somehow he was aware subconsciously when Tazie died many years ago. I promised to find this house they were to share and get it back for him, whatever the cost. He was my beloved grandfather. How could I refuse him that if it was within my power? No-one quite knows what happened when he was a young man in love,' he said. 'But suddenly this house was lost to him, and so was she. Months later he got himself home to Toronto and found a letter waiting for him. She had married another who could support her, and they had gone far away.'

His bitter words hung between them, and she didn't know what to say. It was an old tragedy, but the hurt still lived on in James's grandson. She stooped to retrieve her coffee mug.

'But why does owning a house over here mean so much to him now?'

'You don't understand, Stephanie. He died six months ago.'

'Oh, I'm sorry.'

'Don't be. He was very ill, and we knew he couldn't get better.'

'But if it meant so much to him why didn't he do something about it before?'

'Out of loyalty to my grandmother, but when she died it began to haunt him. He talked a lot about the home he was cheated out of by Tazie's father. It was used as a wager, you see, which my grandfather won, fair and square. It should have been his. It was all arranged, but her father was cruel. He made life impossible. James became ill. That's why he made his will the way he did. I'm his heir, his only living descendant but to inherit, I must acquire the house and show the deeds to his lawyer. That way I get the whole lot, all his real estate, the money, everything.'

'Polmerrick,' she whispered. 'The house is in the village, isn't it?'

She felt suddenly breathless. He nodded

as he put his empty coffee mug down on the deck beside him.

'But why do you have to buy the whole village?'

He stood up and leaned over the rail with his back to her.

'The house is a pearl of great price, the village, too. Polmerrick came on the open market. My intention was to put in a bid for the house in question but Nicholas Ross-lyon refused to sell any property separately.'

Stephanie nodded. She knew that of course, and she began to see what Adam was driving at.

'So by buying the whole place you would get to own the house in question?'

'So I thought at the time. But the house isn't for sale with the village.'

Shocked into chilling silence, Stephanie stared at him. He smiled.

'Do you see now, my love, why I need your help in obtaining the deeds of Harbour Spur?'

'Harbour Spur?' Stephanie exclaimed,

staring at Adam, appalled as he gazed back at her, a half smile on his lips.

'That's right.'

She gasped, trying to still the thumping of her heart.

'But Harbour Spur's been in our family for years. I don't understand.'

She thought suddenly of Adam's calculated expression as he gazed at her grandmother's portrait when he came to cancel his booking.

'It was a shock when I discovered Harbour Spur wasn't included in the sale of Polmerrick. I've got to have that house,' he was insisting.

So that magic time in the cove meant nothing to him? It was all a sham! She thought with pain of the hazy sunshine and the joy that those moments in his arms had given her. A haze of sudden anger blinded her for a second. When it cleared she felt cold inside.

'You brought me here merely to get me to agree to help you get your hands on Harbour Spur, didn't you?' she accused.

'I brought you here?' His eyes laughed at her. 'Wait a minute! It was your idea to stowaway on board my boat.'

She wanted to lash out at him, to wipe that look of calm determination from his face.

'OK, but you were quick to make the most of it.'

Her agony was almost too much to bear. He moved away from her, disappearing down below as if he knew she needed time on her own to come to the right decision. Right for him, of course. If only this numbness would go so that she could think straight. Why did his grandfather think he'd been cheated out of the ownership of her home? It was all a confusion.

CHAPTER SIX

She gazed down over the side at the ridged sand beneath the clear water. Such a short time ago she had swum ashore, delighting in the peaceful cove and the presence of this man who had tricked her so cruelly. She shivered, trying to concentrate on what he had told her. Maybe this numbness was nature's way of helping her bear the way things were. The earlier sense of magic must be working for her in a different way now, leaving her mind blank and her feelings mute for the sake of her sanity.

When Adam returned he looked confident. How incredibly gullible he must think her. It was plain that he would cast her aside immediately he had what he wanted from her. Did he think she didn't realise this now?

'You'll talk to your aunt on my behalf, Stephanie, my love?' he asked, seating himself at her side as if nothing had happened.

'I won't try to persuade her.'

'Not if I offer three times the market price?'

'You'd do that?'

'That, and more.'

'And when she refuses?'

He shrugged.

'My grandfather's money is rightly mine, and I mean to have it. The bank will loan me the money to buy the village to develop. It's a good investment.'

Was there a threat in his words? Of course there was. By developing the place around them, the peace of Harbour Spur would be shattered for ever. Harbour Spur Guesthouse, in the midst of all this, would be forced to change, maybe go out of business. So that was his plan – to force Millie into the position of having to sell whether she liked it or not! She shuddered.

'So,' she said. 'That's your revenge, to

spoil the village for ever?'

'What I intend to do will improve the place.'

He leaned forward and took both her hands in his.

'My love, please understand.'

For a moment she saw in his face the ruthlessness that lay beneath his dynamic charm.

'I want you to explain to her,' he went on.

Stephanie gave a gurgling laugh that had more than a hint of hysteria in it. She could just imagine it – Millie listening sympathetically to this talk about an old love letter and the inheritance, depending on his acquisition of her own beloved home. Oh, yes, Millie would have a field day over that!

Adam leaned forward, and pulled her towards him. With his face so close to hers, it was hard to think coherently. Then he bent his head to kiss her. For a second she seemed to melt into him. Then the wave of reality broke, crashing her down to earth. What was she thinking of? Hc was her enemy. She pulled away angrily. There seemed to be pent-up energy in him now that needed release. He looked around, shading his eyes against the glare of the sun. His dark hair ruffled slightly.

'Wind!' he shouted exultantly. 'It's coming. Look out there on the water.'

She looked, and saw the dark patches rippling slowly towards them across the surface that showed that wind was getting up. Adam immediately went forward to raise the sails in preparation for moving off. As she watched his quick, deft work she marvelled that so short a time ago he was beginning to mean all the world to her. Now she hated him for what he planned to do.

'Take the wheel,' he called back to her as he went forward to pull up the anchor.

She did as he said, relieved that they would soon be on their way out through the arms of the inlet. Then he took over at the helm and she was free to relax. They made good speed to Falmouth. Once out of the inlet the wind had filled the sails satisfactorily, but for

Stephanie, anxious now to escape from Adam, they couldn't go fast enough. When Adam indicated that she should take over the helm again, Stephanie felt so much confidence in herself that she had no hesitation in doing so. She felt, standing at the wheel, that it was in her power to encourage the yacht to greater speed and so end this unbearable situation.

Adam threw himself down on a seat near her, and leaned back with both arms stretched along the rail and his face raised to the sky. She didn't look at him. It was enough that he was near, teasing her senses in spite of all they had been through in the last hour or two. His nearness was intoxicating. So was the knowledge that he trusted her with *Sea Sharon* when soon they would enter the busy Carrick Roads with the town in the distance. It was only when they were edging towards the mooring buoy that Adam sprang up to stand at her side.

'I'll take her now,' he said.

His hands were warm as he touched hers

briefly. His smile lingered in his eyes, and she knew her seamanship impressed him. Yesterday his praise would have warmed her heart, but now all she wanted was to get away from him at the first opportunity.

After that it seemed to be all action as a rubber dinghy came swiftly to them. Seeing it, Adam gave a grunt of satisfaction.

'My crew. Obviously on the look-out and wondering what became of me yesterday.'

They did what was necessary to the sails with practised ease and then all three disappeared below to examine the faulty engine and discuss what should be done. Stephanie, remaining on deck, glanced furtively at the dinghy, wondering if she could make a break for it. She had hardly formulated the thought before Adam was back explaining that the work that had to be done on the faulty engine was likely to take a day or two.

'A day or two?' she echoed.

'I'll send you back to Polmerrick in a taxi, Stephanie.'

'No way. I'm not taking money from you,'

she exploded as he took some notes from his wallet and held them out to her.

He wasn't even prepared to call a taxi for her himself it appeared.

'It's a long walk,' he said. 'Or will you swim?'

His eyes danced at her as she bit her lip, considering. She had only the pound or two she kept in the pocket of her cagoule for emergencies. The money wasn't enough to be much help. There was no choice if she wanted to get back to Polmerrick today.

'Don't be a fool, Stephanie. Take it.'

'The train,' she said at last. 'I'll go on the train.'

It was humiliating enough to be forced to borrow money for her train fare.

'Be sure, I'll repay you as soon as possible,' she insisted.

'I'll hold you to that. It might make all the difference to the purchase money for Harbour Spur.'

She scowled. So he could joke about it now? He smiled, and looked round as if he expected to see a train materialise in front of her.

'I'll find the station, don't worry,' she said.

'Sure? OK then. I'm relying on you, Stephanie. You know what I mean.'

'You must think me a fool. How do I know that you're not spinning me some more yarns?'

The hurt in his eyes nearly finished her, nearly but not quite. She knew about his ruthless determination and she was now on her guard.

'I have an appointment at Rosslyon House next week,' he said. 'Both lawyers will be present. If she wishes, your aunt can examine the plans.'

Not trusting herself to answer, Stephanie picked up her bag and moved off swiftly until *Sea Sharon* was out of sight. Then she looked for a phone box for a call to Millie to tell her not to expect her until noon at the earliest. That done, she headed for the station. She didn't have long to wait.

The movement of the train was so soothing that Stephanie caught herself nodding off to sleep once or twice. Even though it was still only mid-morning enough had happened already to make it seem much later. She yawned, and then smoothed her hair away from her eyes.

It wasn't until she had changed trains at Truro that Stephanie thought seriously about what she was going to say to her aunt.

Millie's expression of sheer incredulity coupled with relief when she saw her would have been amusing at any other time. But today Stephanie had other things on her mind. She paused at the bottom of the steps. Her aunt came running down so fast that she very nearly overbalanced.

'Steady on,' Stephanie said in alarm.

She caught her, letting her sailing bag fall to the ground at her feet.

'Don't rush at things, Millie. I'm not about to disappear.'

'Thank God you're safe!' Millie cried. 'Where were you in the storm last night, girl?'

'Somewhere quite safe. Millie, we've got

to talk.'

Protesting strongly, her aunt allowed herself to be taken indoors, along the passage and out into the small garden at the back. She sat down opposite Stephanie at the picnic table and looked at her in alarm.

'What happened, Stephanie? Where have you been? Tell me, girl.'

'Millie, when did your mother, my grandmother, come back here to Harbour Spur to live?' Stephanie asked before she could say any more. 'I know she lived in London for a while but she came back here to be with her parents for your birth, didn't she? Or have I got that wrong?'

Millie's mouth dropped open.

'What's that got to do with anything?'

'Please, Millie, I need to know.'

Millie rested both elbows on the table and gazed at her niece as if she was mad.

'Why have you got to know that at this particular moment? Where were you last night, Steph?'

Stephanie sighed. She knew she would

have to explain before her aunt would say another word, but she was reluctant to start on something that would enrage Millie and send her blood pressure soaring.

'For goodness' sake, Steph, tell me where you've been.'

There was nothing for it. Stephanie took a deep breath.

'On Adam Hardwicke's boat, the yacht that berths in the harbour sometimes.'

Millie stared at her, astounded.

'You were on board that? Are you stark, raving mad?'

'I didn't mean to be on board. It was accidental.'

'You allowed yourself to fall into that man's clutches by accident? Where did he take you, for goodness' sake?'

'You've got it wrong. It wasn't like that. At least not quite.'

'Then how was it?'

'An error of judgement, that's all.'

'That's all, she says. Whatever possessed you, Steph?'

What had possessed her? Millie was right in implying she must have been out of her mind. At the time it had seemed reasonable to leave the packet for him on board *Sea Sharon*. She tried to explain what happened, but even to her own ears it sounded ridiculous.

'I left it too late to get off *Sea Sharon* because of the falling tide.'

Stephanie could see the dismay in her aunt's face, and spoke quickly.

'We rode out the storm into shelter down the coast. Then this morning we sailed on to Falmouth for the engine to be repaired and I came home by train. Listen, Millie, it was my own fault.'

'I bet he was only too pleased.'

'We talked. He told me about his grandfather's will. There's a condition in it that's important. Adam'll inherit a lot of money if he can get hold of Harbour Spur. That's what it's all about. At least I found that out.'

'But why Harbour Spur? Did you ask him?'

'His grandfather was a Canadian. He was over in this country and fell in love. I suppose he stayed at Harbour Spur, and got to love it.'

'So this Hardwicke man thought all he had to do was snap his fingers and it's his? He spun you a few yarns and you believed him!'

'I don't know what to believe any more.'

She only knew that she couldn't stop loving him now, whatever happened. She was too weak-willed to put this manipulative man out of her mind. She despised herself.

'I see now why he wants to buy Polmerrick,' Millie said triumphantly. 'Revenge, he's out for revenge! Better watch out, girl, or he'll kidnap you for real next time.'

Stephanie was startled. Kidnap! The idea hadn't occurred to her. So why didn't he hang on to her today? It would have been easy enough for someone like Adam to do just that and to demand Harbour Spur as a ransom. She had had a lucky escape, Millie, too.

'It's strange, Steph, but I never could understand why Mother wanted me to have this place after her and not your father. But there, your dad died, and you're here now. It's yours anyway,' Millie was saying.

Stephanie leaned forward and took her hands in her own.

'I know it will be one day, Millie, but not for ages, I hope.'

'You don't understand, Steph. Harbour Spur is yours now. It's all drawn up legally. I thought it best, and I know how much the place means to you.'

Stephanie was speechless. The breath seemed to leave her body. Harbour Spur hers?

'You mean,' she gasped out at last, 'you really mean you've made Harbour Spur over to me, legally?'

'Haven't I just said so, girl? You, Stephanie Polgrean, are the true owner of Harbour Spur.'

CHAPTER SEVEN

Stephanie finished watering the hanging baskets. Then she stood still for a moment, the empty can in her hands. Millie had had her say and then gone storming off indoors. Maybe she shouldn't have told her about Adam's revelations. On the other hand she herself needed to know whether there was the slightest likelihood that Adam might have some element of truth on his side. Only by talking to her aunt could she be sure of that.

'When exactly did Tamar Trevarrick come back to Polmerrick to live permanently?' she had asked Millie again.

'It was soon after the war ended and your father was about two years old and I was twelve. Her father had died by then, and her mother couldn't cope with Harbour Spur on her own. Mother had a hard time of it, but she made this place pay. She made me promise never to let it go out of the family's hands for whatever reason.'

'And there's nothing else? No secret I don't know about?'

'Nothing.'

'We've got to think seriously about the future, Millie. It's got to be said. Suppose anything happened, you became ill, or anything. The money from this place would set you up for the rest of your life. You must think about it.'

Millie laughed.

'Why are you talking like this, girl?'

Stephanie hadn't answered for a moment. She owed her aunt so much. She had to think of her best interests now. The window above her head clattered open. Stephanie looked up to see her aunt leaning out to shake her duster.

'There's a protest meeting organised for next week,' she called down. 'I forgot to tell you, Steph. We'll see what happens then.

Taking over the whole of Polmerrick indeed, whoever heard the like!'

Her head popped back in and the window banged shut. Stephanie took the empty watering can back inside the house. She had just gone into the kitchen when there was a huge crash upstairs. Mrs Luke came running out of one of the front bedrooms as Stephanie flew up the stairs.

'Your aunt,' she gasped. 'She's had an accident. Come quick!'

There was no sound from Millie. Stephanie could see why. The wardrobe had fallen over and her aunt's foot was imprisoned beneath. Millie lay unconscious on her back, her eyes closed. Without a word they both heaved at the wardrobe and moved it off her foot.

'Phone for an ambulance, Mrs Luke, quickly,' Stephanie exclaimed.

Placing a pillow beneath her aunt's head, and a duvet over her was all Stephanie could do for the moment except to talk soothingly and confidently as Millie began to come round. Mrs Luke returned.

'I'll go in the ambulance with her. Find my bag, will you? Get the guests to make their own arrangements for dinner this evening, Mrs Luke, and we'll reimburse them later.'

'That I will. Don't you fret about nothing. I'll stay as long as you want.'

To Stephanie's relief, the ambulance was soon at the door. Stephanie followed anxiously as Millie was carried downstairs on a stretcher. Much later, after X-rays, Stephanie was told that an operation was necessary. They would be keeping her in hospital for a few days.

Stephanie walked out of the hospital's main door in a daze, shivering at the fresh air after the warmth inside. A car drew swiftly to a stop beside her and Adam Hardwicke got out. Stephanie gasped as he took her arm.

'Hop in.'

She felt too weak to resist. He put the car into gear and they moved off.

'When did you last eat?' he asked her.

'I don't know. Breakfast, on *Sea Sharon*, I suppose.'

'Hours ago. We'll find somewhere.'

He drew up at a small pub on the outskirts of town. He ordered sandwiches and coffee for them both, and then sat down at her side. As the warmth began to get to her she thought of Harbour Spur, and the necessity to hurry back for Mrs Luke's sake. She half-rose to her feet.

'Sit down, Stephanie. You can't go anywhere looking like this. The food's coming now,' Adam insisted.

Suddenly she was ravenous. He put down his coffee cup later and smiled.

'Better now?'

Stephanie nodded.

'Tell me about your aunt. How serious is it?'

She looked at him suspiciously, remembering that he had tried to use her once already today. She needed to be on her guard.

'Why do you want to know?'

'Common courtesy. Did you get a chance to put my plans to her?'

'No way! You used me.'

The glint in his eyes was unnerving, and she looked away, remembering the soft feel of the early morning and the love for him that had welled up inside her as he came towards her.

'Do you really believe that of me?'

She didn't want to, oh, how she didn't want to. Her eyes flashed.

'Millie will never sell Harbour Spur. Forget it, and leave us alone.'

'So how serious is your aunt's injury?'

'They'll tell me more when I go back this evening.'

'I'll drive you home and back later.'

'You will not.'

One side of his mouth quirked into a half-smile. She decided to ignore it.

'Did you know that a meeting's being organised, a protest meeting against your threatened take-over of Polmerrick?' she asked instead.

The pent-up energy in the air between them was almost tangible. He seemed to stiffen, and the expression in his eyes was hard.

'Before or after Friday?'

'Friday?' she asked.

'We have a meeting with our lawyers, Rosslyon and myself, to finalise details before contracts are exchanged.'

'I've forgotten. You should be at our meeting, to hear the reaction to your plans to ruin the place.'

'How likely is Rosslyon to listen to the villagers at this stage when they didn't come into his calculations before?'

'How should I know? But most of the villagers are very angry and worried.'

He looked determined.

'I need to put my ideas across strongly so they all agree it's for the best.'

'You're very sure of yourself.'

'Oh, boy, I am. I can take all the time I need. My business back home is in the hands of someone I can trust, and I'm in constant touch. So you can see, modern technology holds no fears for me. I'm quite handy on the telephone, too, which is how I knew about your aunt's accident, by the way, and that you were at the hospital with her.'

'So Mrs Luke told you.'

She looked anxious.

'I've got to go.'

He stood up, and pulled her up with him. His nearness set her senses aflame. It was hard to remember that this was all a game to him, a ruse to get his own way.

'You've had just about enough today, my love,' he murmured as they emerged into bright sunlight. 'When the engine's fixed, *Sea Sharon* will be on a permanent berth in Polmerrick harbour while negotiations are taking place. I'll be there should you need me.'

She gave a strangled laugh, and the breath caught in her throat.

'Need you? The last person we need about the place is you.'

He smiled grimly to himself as they moved towards the car.

'I'll drive you to the hospital later. How soon, a couple of hours?'

'I'm driving myself.'

'I'll be here to drive you, so be ready.'

Too exhausted to argue, she said no more, resolved to allow nothing of the kind.

To see Millie sitting up in bed was a pleasant surprise. Stephanie smiled as she bent to kiss her aunt, holding out her spray of pink roses wordlessly.

'Now don't get emotional, Steph,' Millie said as she took them and buried her face in their scent. 'Such beautiful roses. Are you watering my hanging baskets?'

Stephanie laughed, and wiped the tears from her eyes.

'That's better, Steph. I'm the one who should be in tears doing such a fool thing with that wardrobe.'

'But you feel better now the operation's over? I popped in for a bit yesterday but they said you were resting.'

'I'll be all right, girl. Home soon, I hope.'

'We'll see.'

Millie leaned back on her pillow, looking

at her niece anxiously.

'You're managing all right at home, Steph?'

'We're OK. The guests seem content. They sent their love.'

Stephanie, looking around the pleasant ward, wasn't aware at first of the nurse approaching Millie's bed with a huge basket of flowers. At her aunt's gasp of pleasure she looked at the basket in the nurse's arms.

'They're magnificent,' Millie cried. 'The scent of these carnations! But who are they from?'

She examined the card then exclaimed, 'Nick Rosslyon!'

'Nick?' Stephanie exclaimed.

Millie gave a laugh.

'Too beautiful for the likes of me. They should be for you, Steph. Maybe that's what he intended.'

'Rubbish, Millie. He always thought a lot of you.'

After about an hour, Stephanie left, promising to be back next day. Deep in thought she drove the mile or two into Truro. She had no need to be back in Polmerrick just yet, and she had shopping to do. She parked the car, still thinking of Nick Rosslyon's grand gesture in sending the flowers to Millie. Maybe the guilt about selling Polmerrick was beginning to get to him. Surely she needn't read any more into it than that? But she knew that Millie's suspicions that he was still interested in herself might be well-founded.

The things she needed to get were soon purchased. Then she lingered, window shopping, on her way back to the car. Glancing up, she saw someone she knew, instantly recognisable in her flowing shirt and long skirt. She was clutching a large jar of coffee.

'Dinah! Great to see you,' Stephanie said, smiling.

'You, too, Steph. What are you doing here?'

'I could ask you that. I thought you were immersed in work at that studio of yours.'

Dinah grinned.

'So I have been. And now, guess what? I'm

having an exhibition of my stuff here very soon. Crazy, isn't it?'

'Not a bit, Dinah. Your work's good.'

'And you?'

'Visiting Millie. She's in hospital.'

'Heavens, what for?'

'An accident with a wardrobe. It fell on her and injured her ankle.'

'Oh, poor Millie. You've time for a coffee or something?'

Dinah waved her jar of coffee.

'Lucky I popped out for this. Come on, Steph. This way.'

Dinah led her into a small, cobbled street near the cathedral, and up a narrow alleyway. Stephanie saw a new noticeboard painted in bright red and yellow on which black lettering announced the forthcoming exhibition by local artist, Dinah Penberthy.

'Oh, Dinah! It's great, truly it is.'

Her friend gazed up at the board, her face flushed with pleasure.

'I've waited a long time for this. And it's you and Millie I've got to thank. I'd never have done it without your encouragement.'

She found a key in the pocket of her voluminous skirt and opened the door to reveal a surprisingly large room. She looked round proudly at the piles of stacked paintings leaning against the walls. One or two had already been hung, and a pair of steps leaned against the far wall. Stephanie started to examine the ones on display.

'You should be proud of these, Dinah.'

'I've started sorting out, but there are more to come. I've got a chap helping but he's had to go off this afternoon. Right then, coffee! Then you can tell mc all about everything.'

Stephanie sat down on a rather rickety, wooden chair. Dinah handed her an enormous mug, hooked a stool forward with one foot and sat down herself. Confiding in Dinah was a relief Stephanie hadn't looked for. She told her about her visit to Rosslyon House expecting to see Nick's mother. Then she hesitated for a moment.

'And?'

'What would you do, Dinah, if you had the chance to save Polmerrick from being sold to a developer?'

'Depends on the catch.'

'It does, doesn't it?'

Her own thoughts exactly. Too big a catch she had thought at the time. Now she wondered if she had been too sharp with Nick.

'Mmm. Sounds as if it's a big one,' Dinah observed.

'Marriage to Nick Rosslyon.'

'Wow! That's crazy.'

'You really think so?'

'I know so. Steph. He asked you then? What did you say?'

'I refused him.'

'Good for you.'

'You never liked him, did you, Dinah?'

'Too full of himself, that one. What sort of man would try to buy himself a woman, tell me that?'

Nick would try, Stephanie thought. Adam, too, but Adam was wanting to do it the other way round, or something similar. Between the two of them Polmerrick was being used, as well as herself. She frowned.

'It's blackmail,' Dinah said firmly. 'I'm glad you told Nick Rosslyon where to go!'

'But you see, there's Harbour Spur.'

'Don't tell me he's got designs on Harbour Spur, too?'

'Not Nick, someone else.'

'Steph, what do you mean?' Dina asked, wide-eyed.

'The man who wants to buy Polmerrick wants Harbour Spur, too.'

'In heaven's name why?'

'Something about Harbour Spur meaning a lot to his grandfather.'

'His grandfather? What's he got to do with anything? Come on, Steph. Tell me everything! It all sounds ludicrous to me.'

Stephanie looked at her friend, and knew she had to unburden herself to someone. Everything she said would be safe with Dinah.

'He made it a condition that if his grandson wanted to inherit his fortune he had to first acquire Harbour Spur.'

'It's crazy.'

Stephanie shrugged, remembering the love letter, but somehow she couldn't come out with the information about that. In some strange way it was personal.

'Has this man a name?' Dinah asked.

'Adam Hardwicke. He seems to think there was some injustice connected with Harbour Spur, that it should have been his. But our family has owned it for years.'

'A made-up story then? Unscrupulous.'

Stephanie considered.

'He believes it's true.'

Dinah got up and started to prowl round the room. Stephanie said nothing for a while. She sipped her coffee, grateful for the comforting warmth. It was comforting, too, that her friend was so against her marrying Nick for any reason at all.

CHAPTER EIGHT

Millie's homecoming a few days later was a matter for rejoicing, and she made the most of it. Ensconced in her own room she ordered the life of the guesthouse as if she was preparing battlelines. One evening Stephanie heard the telephone ring and then her aunt's enraged tones. She rushed into the room.

'Who?' Millie cried. 'You mean to say you want to speak to my niece? Well, you can't. She wants nothing to do with you, that's why not. I'd know that accent anywhere. You can't fool me. How dare you! Important? What's important at this time of night I should like to know?'

Stephanie rushed over.

'Who is it?'

The outraged expression on her aunt's

face told her.

'I won't talk to him,' she cried, her heart pounding.

'Get off the line,' Millie snapped, and slammed the phone down.

Stephanie had hardly let out her long, agonised breath when the phone rang again. This time Millie didn't wait to hear who it was, but put the receiver straight down.

When it rang for the third time Stephanie cried, 'He won't give up. I'll take it downstairs.'

She rushed headlong down to the hall, half expecting Millie to hang up on him again in her wrath. She had to stop this. His voice sounded so close, so warm, that tears sprang to her eyes. She didn't want to hear from him, but his voice had the power to set her heart trembling.

'You, Adam?' she asked into the receiver.

'I've been concerned about you, Stephanie,' the reply came.

There was the sound of a snort on the line.

'Put the phone down, Millie,' Stephanie ordered. 'At once, d'you hear?'

Adam gave a sound like suppressed mirth. Stephanie said nothing more until she heard the click of the receiver being replaced upstairs.

'As I said, I've been concerned. How are things going with you?'

His voice sounded kindly sympathetic, but how could she trust him? She hardened her voice.

'Adam, I meant it when I asked you to get out of my life and stay out.'

The effort it cost her to say those words was immense. As she replaced the receiver she felt her unhappiness like a dead weight. Only then did she wonder why it was so important to him to phone her at this hour. Would be try again? It seemed not. So she had got through to him at last.

So much had been happening at Harbour Spur that Stephanie almost forgot the protest meeting. She and Mrs Luke had had their usual busy day seeing to the guests as well as attempting to obey Millie's every whim. Stephanie's heart gave a jolt as Mrs Luke began to speak about the meeting.

'You ought to be there, I say, m'dear. It's only right.'

Stephanie shook her head.

'It's all a lot of fuss about nothing,' Mrs Luke said. 'What good's it doing letting the place go to rack and ruin when there's someone willing to put his hand in his pocket and set things to rights?'

Stephanie began to chop watercress as if her life depended on it.

'But that's not all he plans to do,' she said earnestly. 'Do you really want Polmerrick changed, Mrs Luke, the place you grew up in?'

'But he can't change it all that much, m'dear.'

'I think he could.'

'He don't look the type.'

Stephanie looked at her in astonishment. It just showed how easily Adam Hardwicke could turn on the charm at will and deceive people into doing and believing exactly what he wanted. Mrs Luke looked at her closely.

'You seem to be taking this very hard, m'dear. I've seen you talking to him once or twice. A fine couple you made and all. It's a shame.'

Why did her heart lurch so horribly? With a supreme effort, Stephanie concentrated on the watercress, at the same time doing her best to take in what Mrs Luke was saying.

'I don't know what's got into your aunt, minding about him so much. Just as well she's got to stay here and can't get there to stir things up. There'd be fireworks then and no mistake.'

'She feels as strongly about it all as I do,' Stephanie said.

Mrs Luke grunted.

'All I want is my cottage roof mended, and I'll be satisfied, but tell that to Nick Rosslyon's deaf ears and see where it gets you!'

On the following Friday, Stephanie's mind was filled with the knowledge that today

Adam and his solicitor were due to meet Nick Rosslyon and his legal man. Her thoughts were so bemused she wasn't surprised to see Nick himself on the doorstep when she went to open it when the doorbell rang.

'How's your aunt?' he asked abruptly as he followed her inside.

He looked ill-at-ease as he seated himself at one end of the large sofa and sat with his legs apart, a hand on each knee. Stephanie sat down on a hard chair opposite him.

'You can see for yourself in a minute.'

Nick flushed slightly.

'It's you I came to see, Steph.'

She looked at him enquiringly.

'I don't know how to say this, but Mother thinks … well, we plan to hold the Regatta Ball at Rosslyon House this year as a sort of farewell to Polmerrick people. Do you think that's a good idea, Steph?'

'You're definitely leaving Polmerrick then?'

Nick smiled, looking pleased with himself.

'There's someone else interested now as

well as Hardwicke.'

'But Adam…'

'Adam now, is it?'

Stephanie flushed.

'Mr Hardwicke's determined to have the village. Why have you really come here, Nick?'

'I told you, the ball. I wanted to know what you thought, Steph. Mother thinks we can get things organised quickly. Will you come, Steph?'

She nodded absently, her thoughts on Adam. What would he do in this added complication of another person wanting Polmerrick? Did he even know about it?

'Are you going to tell Adam Hardwicke about this other interest?'

'Why should I?'

Nick looked at her anxiously, his pale forehead puckered.

'What's wrong, Steph?'

She shook her head.

'Your aunt's all right, isn't she? Could you bring her up to see Mother? She could help in the plans, if she could,' Nick went on.

'Plans?'

'For the ball. Mother wants her to come and talk about it if she's up to it.'

Stephanie stared out the window at the harbour and the colour-washed cottages on the other side. The loveliness of the familiar scene was an ache. She turned to Nick again.

'What's going to happen to Polmerrick?'

'How should I know?'

'Do you even care?'

He hesitated for a moment, and then spoke with a rush.

'You can still stop it, you know, Steph, by saying just one word.'

So it had come to this in the end, as she had known it would. She moved to the door without answering him.

'I'll see if Millie's awake. She'll want to see you.'

'Steph, please, listen to me.'

'I can't, Nick. It's out of the question. And now I've got things to do. I'll have to go.'

'But you think it's a good idea, the Regatta

Ball at Rosslyon House?'

'See what Millie thinks. I'll take you up to her now.'

She left them to it. She had no wish to talk any more with Nick, and she needed a breath of air. There were only a few people on the beach as she walked to the rocks on the other side. Today the sea surged darkly and there were hints of white horses far out on the choppy water. Seating herself on a rock, she stared out to sea, the breeze whipping her hair across her face. She felt drained. Wheeling above the cliffs the sea birds called sorrowfully, suiting her mood. She closed her eyes.

It could have been hours later, or merely minutes that she opened them again. Far out, a yacht was heeling over in the grey sea. No other vessel could slice the waves as *Sea Sharon* could, or look so magnificent approaching shore. She got to her feet, heart thumping, wanting desperately to watch the arrival. But instead she hurried back to the safety of Harbour Spur.

Staring back at her from the hall mirror was a pale face with wide, unhappy eyes. The ring of the doorbell made her jump. On the doorstep was a girl. She looked dazzling.

'Adam said to give you this.'

Stephanie took the envelope and held it in her hand. She knew what it was of course – the love letter James Hardwicke had written to his true love, Tazie. She stared at the packet with a stirring of anger that rose in her throat and made her dizzy. Adam Hardwicke was deliberately pressurising her, putting her under an intolerable strain as part of his plan to get his hands on Harbour Spur. It seemed he would never give up.

She took a deep breath, struggling for calm as she closed the door again. Her first thought was to destroy the letter at once if Adam thought so little of something he should have valued. But it had been written in love with no thought of anyone other than the young girl. She couldn't do it. She looked round for somewhere to hide it. Adam wanted her to look after it, and she would, but she wouldn't read it again. It brought too many painful memories she could well do without. Slipping it into the drawer in the telephone table, she went outside with the watering can to attend to the hanging baskets before they dried out.

Stephanie was in the hall that evening when the telephone rang. Lifting the receiver she recognised Dinah's cheerful voice.

'Listen to this, Steph. I had to find a phone box at once to tell you. Nick Rosslyon found my exhibition, came in and insisted I accept his special invitation to the Regatta Ball. What do you think of that? I was gobsmacked, too. Good old Nick. Never misses a chance, does he?'

Stephanie smiled.

'So, did you accept?'

'What d'you think? Wouldn't miss it for the world. You are going to it, Steph? I'm relying on you being there. I know you want to avoid Nick, but…'

'I'm glad you're coming, too, Dinah.'

'Good. I trust I'll get a bed for the night at

Harbour Spur.'

'When have we ever refused you?'

'I know, I know. Just checking. I'll be there at the ball, to protect you, Steph, OK?'

In the days that followed, Stephanie had good reason to be grateful for Nick's suggestion that Millie help his mother in the planning of the Regatta Ball. This occupied the sedentary Millie's thoughts as nothing else could have done. Even the thought of the proposed takeover was pushed to the back of their minds. Stephanie tried hard to take her cue from her aunt's enthusiasm for the ball and enter into some of the discussions.

She managed avoiding seeing Nick alone each time he brought his mother to see Millie. Everyone in Polmerrick was invited, and the organisation for such a huge event was enormous. Once or twice she drove Millie to Rosslyon House without seeing Nick. She heard no more of other prospective purchasers of the village from the Rosslyons, or anything of Adam going ahead with the deal either.

Unlike her employer, Mrs Luke had nothing like that to occupy her. Her talk was all of the sale of the village and how things had cropped up to complicate matters and prevent her cottage roof being repaired. Rumours were rife, and Mrs Luke knew them all.

Stephanie had tried hard to stem the flow the first morning after *Sea Sharon* had returned to Polmerrick, but soon realised that nothing she could say would make any difference. It was better to let her old friend have her head and to try to blot out her words and concentrate instead on their guests' needs.

Preparations for the ball at Rosslyon House went ahead smoothly. Even Stephanie felt a stir of interest as the day approached. Dinah arrived in the afternoon, parking her old van in the yard at the back and staggering in through the kitchen with her large suitcase.

'It's huge, I know,' she gasped. 'But it's the only one I've got.'

'Here, let me,' Stephanie said, taking it from her. 'Come on upstairs.'

Dinah, going ahead of her, stopped on the landing and looked up at the portrait.

'A fine artist that, Steph. Look at the sea behind her. You can almost feel the surge of it. And what character in her face even though she's so young. She could have told you a thing or two, I bet.'

Stephanie sighed.

'I wish she hadn't died before I was born. I used to ask Millie about her when I was little. I used to love her stories of what Harbour Spur was like in the old days. It all seemed so happy. But it couldn't have been really. She had a hard time of it making a go of it.'

'I bet. I wonder why she didn't sell?'

'She loved the place,' Stephanie said dreamily.

'So it was worth all the grind?'

'Millie thought so.'

'And you?'

'Oh, yes. If you have a dream you must

hang on to it. It's like you and that cottage of yours, Dinah. A lot of people would think you crazy.'

Her friend laughed as they continued upwards.

'I think so myself sometimes.'

Dinah's room was on the floor above, a small one overlooking the harbour. She took her case from Stephanie and put it on the bed to open.

'Now go away, Stephanie. It's a surprise, what I'm going to wear tonight.'

Stephanie laughed.

'I can't wait. See you downstairs.'

That night, Millie looked at her niece approvingly as Stephanie came downstairs.

'That green suits you, Steph. I hadn't realised before how like my mother you are.'

'Tamar?'

Startled, Stephanie glanced back at the portrait.

'If only! You look very good yourself, Millie.'

Her aunt snorted at the compliment.

'No-one looks good with their left foot in plaster and their right foot in a flat sandal.'

Stephanie laughed.

'That's better, Steph. We're not going to a funeral.'

'Where's Dinah?'

'Waiting for us in the sitting-room.'

Stephanie heard voices and laughter as she opened the door. Dinah was swirling round in a full, glittering skirt, egged on by the elderly couple who had arrived for their stay in Harbour Spur that morning. They turned happy faces towards her.

'Doesn't she look stunning?' Millie said.

'She certainly does,' Stephanie replied.

'Are we all set? Come on then. Cheerio, folks. Tell you all about it tomorrow,' Dinah said as they left the room.

Millie raised herself awkwardly from the hall chair and allowed Stephanie to help her out to the car. They arrived deliberately early for Millie's sake. The chandeliers at the hall shone with a brilliance that was reflected in the long wall mirrors as Stephanie escorted her aunt to the dais on which Nick's mother had seated herself in readiness to view the proceedings. A chair and footstool had been placed there for Millie.

Nick himself was resplendent in tuxedo, looking faintly astonished that he was actually here at all among the villagers and tenants he had effected to despise. He came forward to greet Stephanie as soon as she had seen Millie settled. She looked round for Dinah, but couldn't see her.

'Your friend has made herself at home,' Nick said, looking pleased with himself. 'And I've told someone to look after her. Don't worry about her.'

'I'm not. Dinah can look after herself.'

'You look beautiful, Steph!'

He took her hand and led her on to the dance floor. As the evening progressed, Stephanie danced with others, too, though Nick always claimed her immediately afterwards. He left her once or twice in order to do his duty but always returned. Dinah waved to her once or twice as she swirled past with yet another partner. Stephanie couldn't help a little feeling of premonition as she looked round at the people enjoying themselves with such gusto. Not so long ago these same people had been raising objections about the Rosslyon family selling out. Had Adam charmed them so easily?

CHAPTER NINE

At supper time Nick devoted himself entirely to Stephanie, filling her plate with delicacies, and plying her with glasses of an excellent dry white wine that briefly revived her flagging spirits. All she wanted now was to sit out the rest of the evening. Nick's attentions were becoming an embarrassment, and she was afraid he had been drinking too heavily.

He found seats for them out in the rose garden. Other guests were wandering about admiring the herbaceous borders, but here they were alone. He placed his empty glass on the grass, and leaned so close the could smell his breath.

'Steph,' he said earnestly, 'you know how I feel. Together we could make a go of this place. I'd pull out of anything for you. You know I would.'

'How can you pull out now, Nick? It's not possible.'

'I'll pull out of anything for your sake, Steph.'

She didn't know how to answer him, to make him realise for good that she meant what she said. As she tried to think, a faint warning of a footfall on grass seeped into her consciousness.

'You won't pull out of the sale of Polmerrick!'

Her heart leaped to her throat at the sound of Adam's voice. Nick sprang up. Adam stood there, magnificent in black suit and white shirt. His strong shoulders seemed to strain his jacket as he took a step towards Stephanie and pulled her to her feet. For a moment their eyes met and held.

It was impossible to fathom what lay behind the expressionless gaze. That he was angry was painfully obvious. With her? It seemed that he was because no smile reached his eyes.

'What do you mean by this?' Nick blustered. 'Where have you come from? You weren't invited. Get out at once or...'

'Or nothing.'

Adam's voice was like steel as he let go of Stephanie's hands.

'I've come for what's rightfully mine, and I'm not talking about Polmerrick.'

Stephanie moved away from him. She let out a little sigh, and a shiver ran through her. In the dim light she saw Nick's face redden.

'Then what are we talking about? There's nothing here for you now, so get out.'

'The sale of Polmerrick was tied up legally this morning, as well you know. So we'll have no loose talk about pulling out of anything, d'you hear, Rosslyon?'

All the stuffing seemed to go out of Nick as he looked at Stephanie helplessly.

'I wasn't ... I mean...'

She could almost feel sorry for him. No-one could stand up against Adam in this mood or in any other. She stood between them, pale and silent, knowing that words must break the situation but still unable to frame them. It was Nick who spoke.

'Steph, you don't want him here? Just say the word.'

Adam shrugged disdainfully. He stared at her with cool appraisal.

'We need to talk.'

'No,' she said faintly. 'It's finished. You have Polmerrick. Be satisfied with that.'

'I shall not be satisfied until I've got what I came for, and more.'

'Leave Harbour Spur alone, can't you?' Stephanie said. 'There's nothing more to be said.'

'Oh, but there is.'

She raised startled eyes to his. Adam smiled, and the grim lines left the corners of his mouth for a moment.

'I made a promise to my grandfather, an important one. It involves you, Stephanie. That's why we have to talk.'

'You're wrong. No way can it involve me. We've said all we need to say on the subject.'

Nick took a belligerent step forward.

'I'm not going to be threatened on my own property.'

'Yours?'

'Mine,' Nick said firmly but his hands trembled. 'This is my place, until we complete the sale.'

Stephanie didn't know what he would do, but she had to stop him whatever it was. She put out a restraining hand.

'It's all right, Nick. I'll come back in with you now.'

Adam eyed her coldly.

'A few moments only, in private, if you please.'

'I've nothing more to say.'

Nick, with his arm round her, was all boldness again.

'I told you, Hardwicke. Harbour Spur could never be in the deal. Can't you see Steph doesn't want all this hassle? Come on, love, we're going.'

To her surprise, Adam stood back. She expected him to order her to remain, but he allowed her to be led away. His cool authority as he stood looking at her was unnerving. She hadn't heard the last of this, she knew.

The noise of chatter inside the house rattled round in her head. Nick was wanted in the dining-room, much to her relief, and she was able to go to the dais in the ball-room unescorted. Her aunt was there alone, and she sat down beside her.

She couldn't begin to imagine why Adam wanted to talk to her so urgently when he had said all that needed to be said. Too late, she remembered the packet he had wanted to be in her safekeeping. A curious empti-ness pressed on her spirits. She struggled to concentrate on what Millie was telling her about her recent conversation with Mrs Rosslyon. There was something about a new flat overlooking the Thames and her being glad that Rosslyon House was to be kept as a family home by the new owner.

'It's all very well for her,' Millie said. 'She'll be out of it. We're the ones to bear the brunt of all the changes, if he gets plan-ning permission, that is. But I said nothing to spoil things, poor lady.'

Stephanie let her talk. The scene in front of her as the band took up its position again and the dancers covered the floor, was cheerful. She was glad that Dinah had stayed inside the house during the interval and had not been a witness to the scene in the garden. She could see Dinah now, still with the same man she had been with from the beginning. Catching her glance, her friend gave a cheerful wave.

Stephanie waved back. At least one of them was having a good time. All she wanted for herself was for the evening to end. Adam had vanished as if it had been all a dream, or a nightmare, and even Nick was busy else-where and did not reappear for her until the last dance was announced. As the dance finished Nick held on to her tightly.

'Don't go, Stephanie. Mother's going to make a speech.'

'A speech?'

The triumphant look was back again.

'You'll see.'

A roll of drums silenced everyone. Mrs Rosslyon, back on the dais now, stood up. She looked a regal figure in her soft grey dress as she began to thank everyone who had helped to make the evening a success. Then others spoke, too, bidding her a last farewell. Stephanie thought it would never end. Nick's fingers were tight on her wrist. Then he let her go suddenly and leaped up beside his mother.

'The last time we were all gathered here it was to make an announcement,' he said. 'You have all heard what happened about that. But tonight I would have liked to make another, but it was not to be. The lady in question is not quite ready, or so she says. But I would like you all to know how dear she is to me, and how very much I hope…'

Stephanie could stand no more. She dare not look at Millie. Seeing the stunned expression on Dinah's face she signalled frantically to her. Fortunately all eyes were on Nick standing so proudly beside his mother. Dinah caught hold of her hand and together

162

they slipped out of the room.

'Did you hear that!' Dinah gasped when they were outside in the hall, heading for the front door. 'Quick, outside before they start to come out.'

She propelled Stephanie to where she had parked her car.

'Give me the keys. I'll drive. You're in no fit state,' Dinah insisted.

Stephanie was trembling as she got into the car.

'Where are we going?'

'To Harbour Spur as fast as I can get you there. Then I'll go back for Millie. She won't be ready for some time with all the fussing. It's great she's being appreciated, but we can't wait.'

She slammed the car into gear.

'You didn't agree to anything?'

'No way.'

'The little rat!'

Much later, lying sleeplessly in her bed, the events of the evening filled Stephanie's mind to overflowing. Round and round in her mind went everything that had happened at Rosslyon House.

Why couldn't Nick understand that she wished to have nothing more to do with him? Surely she had been blunt enough even for Nick to understand. The humiliating scene at the end she would simply not think about. Thank goodness Dinah had been there to whisk her away.

Round and round went the memory of Adam and Nick facing each other on the moonlit lawn. The fury that blazed from Adam seemed to light up the surrounding air and almost seemed to crackle. She could almost feel sorry for Nick. All he had done was to invite her outside in the cool of the evening and had tried to make her change her mind about marrying him, and what business was it of Adam's anyway that he should gatecrash the ball and try to interfere?

Late as it was, there were only a few hours to get through before morning. She must be thankful for that. Turning over yet again she tried hard to compose herself for sleep. But it simply wouldn't come. On impulse, she slipped out of bed and out on to the landing, careful to make no sound that would disturb the others. There was enough glimmering moonlight for her to move silently down to the lower landing. Tamar Trevarrick's portrait was in shadow, but something made Stephanie glance up at it. The artist had given her grandmother's eyes a wisdom she had always found helpful in moments of stress. She wanted badly to see the picture closely again at this moment.

She reached up to lift it from the wall, to carry downstairs. It wasn't until the hall light was on that she saw that the back of the frame had worn loose over the years and there was something inside. She pulled it out and opened up the thin booklet with trembling fingers. She saw at once that it was some sort of daily record Tamar had kept for a few weeks as a young girl. In mounting excitement Stephanie realised what she was reading – an account of her tumultuous love affair with the artist and all about him winning Harbour Spur from her father in a game of cards! Was that possible? Possible, but surely not legally binding? She simply didn't know.

This was something Millie hadn't known, or anyone else either. It was an incredible piece of history. She carried the portrait and the notebook into the kitchen, and propped the portrait against the wall on one of the units so she could see it. Then she sat down at the table for a closer look at the notebook. She read about Tamar's agony at being parted from her artist lover when her parents sent him away on some charge she knew was false. How unthinking, how cruel! Then came the knowledge that she was pregnant. Stephanie gave a little gasp. Oh, poor Tamar! A terrible situation to be in all those years ago. How did she manage?

But her grandmother had had two children only, Millie and her own father, John, ten years later. Quickly she looked at the date that headed the entry. There could be no doubt! The artist was in fact Millie's father!

For some moments, stunned with this knowledge, Stephanie sat quite still. Then, hearing sounds from upstairs, she opened the kitchen door and went into the hall. She looked up as the landing light flashed on. Her aunt stood there in her dressing-gown, leaning on one crutch.

'It's only me,' Stephanie said hastily, going up to join her.

'Frightening anyone out of their wits!' Millie said in an angry whisper.

Stephanie went with her to her bedroom.

'I've got something important to show you, Millie.'

'Can't it wait till morning? What time is it, girl?'

'Time to show you what I found. Wait, please.'

She ran lightly downstairs, picked up portrait and notebook, and hurried back to Millie's room with them. She sat on the end of the bed to show her. It was some moments before Millie looked up, and then she was smiling.

'Hidden there all those years, and I never knew it.'

'She never said anything? Perhaps she forgot she had hidden it there.'

'Could be. It's wonderful to read the words written in her own hand.'

'You recognise it, Millie?'

Her aunt smiled.

'Of course I do, Steph. She was my mother. There was something about that portrait. I used to romanticise about it as a young girl, you know, something about the artist being a prince in disguise, that sort of thing. Mother would never say who he was, you see.'

'So you asked her?'

'Now and again, I plagued her about it, but she would never tell me.'

'He must have been special, don't you think?'

'Oh, yes, and a talented, young man. I wonder what became of him?'

Stephanie picked up the portrait and looked at it closely again.

'To think this picture was hiding a secret

all these years.'

'She didn't tell me till she was dying that entering John's father's name on my birth certificate was her own father's doing when he registered my birth. So I've known, you see, that your dad and I had different fathers, but I never knew that it was my father who painted her portrait. There's no signature on it. I'd give anything to know who he was.'

She looked down at the diary with a wry smile.

'He called her Tazie.'

'Tazie?' Stephanie said, startled. 'How do you know that?'

'It says so here, look.'

Stephanie took the notebook from her. Sure enough, down in one corner was the name Tazie. A shimmer of disbelief ran through her.

'No-one else called her that,' Millie said softly. 'I expect it was his private name for her.'

'I suppose it must have been.'

Stephanie had to think, to take in the implications. She needed time. Millie gave a gigantic yawn.

'Sorry, love, I'm all in. All this excitement is almost too much. I'm glad you told me at once, though. Clever girl to find it. Leave it all now, Steph, and get off to bed. We'll talk about it in the morning.'

'I'll put the portrait back on the wall,' Stephanie said, getting up. 'May I take the notebook to bed with me?'

'D'you need to ask, girl?'

Stephanie smiled, and bent to kiss her.

'Good-night then, Millie. Sleep well.'

She gave Tamar a long, searching look as she replaced the portrait on the wall. No wonder her grandmother looked wise and knowing. No-one guessed what had been hidden there all these years, but she must have wanted the truth to be discovered one day or she wouldn't have put the notebook there in the first place.

Stephanie went back to her own room, and settled herself in bed. Impossible now to think of sleeping ... Tazie, oh, Tazie. The problem now was what to do about what she had discovered.

CHAPTER TEN

Stephanie sprang out of bed and rushed downstairs. Then, heart pounding, she felt in the drawer for Adam's packet. She could remember every single word that Adam's grandfather had written to his Tazie. Was she also Tamar? But Stephanie needed to see it again in black and white.

She opened the letter with trembling hands. The implications were immense. Adam's grandfather was in fact the artist who had painted her own grandmother at Polmerrick all those years ago. Millie, the child of that union, didn't suspect the truth, she was sure of that. So was Millie Adam's aunt as well as her own? Yes, of course. But she and Adam weren't related because her father and Millie didn't share the same father. How on earth was she going to tell

Millie all this, as she surely must?

Tamar must have believed that what she did was for the sake of her child. She had forsaken her young artist lover and married another. No way was Millie's natural father coming back from Canada to claim her once he knew that. All that Tamar had left, apart from her baby, was her portrait that had hung up there on the wall ever since. She must have known she would never see her true love again.

It was his grandson, Adam Hardwicke, who had vowed to return in his place to claim what he considered his. Adam had told her the truth. The notebook had confirmed that. Stephanie looked down at the letter once more.

My dearest love, I shall be far away but you are forever in my thoughts, dear Tazie. Nothing shall part us ever again in this life once I return to claim you, my love, my perfect love. I know you will wait for me for ever.

But Tamar hadn't waited. Life was different in those days, attitudes harsher. What anguish must she have suffered knowing she was pregnant and waiting for her young lover in time? Day after day and no word, until at last she knew she wouldn't be able to keep the expected baby a secret any longer. Did her parents throw her out when she told them? Millie had said she had been born in London and so was her little brother, her own father, ten years later. Tamar returned to Polmerrick and Harbour Spur only when her parents died, to live and work there until she, too, died.

So sad, so terribly sad. How easy it was to make decisions that had consequences down the years that no-one could possibly predict. Stephanie wiped her eyes, and struggled to control more tears that welled up in their place. It was hard to imagine exactly how it was, but she knew enough now to recognise it for the truth. Tamar had wanted Millie to inherit Harbour Spur and not Millie's brother, John, because John was no blood relation to Millie's natural father.

At last Stephanie folded the letter and

replaced it in the packet and took it up to her own room for safe keeping. Millie must know nothing about this until she herself had time to think.

When the dark gradually lightened into dawn Stephanie fell into a troubled sleep. But the movement of people in the house woke her when it was time to get up. She rose, bleary-eyed, to see to the guests' breakfasts. She dare not think what she was going to do, but concentrated on frying bacon and eggs as if her life depended on it.

Dinah came down early to help. Then, while eating her own meal, she described to all who would listen exactly how it had been at the ball last night. Stephanie smiled with the others, relieved that there was no mention of the humiliating scene at the end. Millie didn't say anything about it either when she hobbled down to join them.

'I'm off to Truro now,' Dinah said getting up at last. 'I've promised to get back in good time.'

'Of course, Dinah, your exhibition. I want

to come and see it soon.'

'You bet, Steph. I wouldn't let you get away without a visit to swell the crowds.'

'Us, too,' one of the elderly lady guests said.

Dinah laughed and blew them all a kiss as she left the room.

'And you need to get some colour in your cheeks,' Millie said when Stephanie came back after seeing her friend off. 'No-one would think you were the belle of the ball last night.'

Stephanie smiled.

'Hardly that. What about Dinah?'

'What about her? Having a good time, I grant you that, but it was you Nick Rosslyon wanted. He made that plain enough. And why was that Hardwicke man there in the room at the end, tell me that?'

'Adam appeared in the ballroom?'

'That's what I said.'

Stephanie stared at her aunt, appalled.

'Are you sure?'

'Of course I'm sure. There's nothing

wrong with my eyes even if I've got a bad ankle. The man was there just at the end when Nick was speaking.'

'So he heard everything Nick said?'

'He did indeed, and with a face as thunderous as they come. I thought that's why you left so suddenly, Steph.'

Stephanie bit her lip. But, really, what did it matter? It was nothing to do with her what Nick Rosslyon chose to come out with at the end of the evening. Adam hadn't been invited anyway. All she wanted now was to get some order to her thoughts.

'I think I'll go for a sail,' she said abruptly.

In spite of everything it felt good to be out on the water again. The sky was thin-veiled with a light covering of cloud through which the sun shimmered. She took a deep breath of salty air. Above her, seagulls wheeled and called. She had a decision to make and she didn't know yet how she was going to make it. She needed time and space to work something out.

The wind rose as she left the shelter of the harbour wall. There was enough now to take her out into the bay at a fair speed. This was her place and she was doing what she loved best. She was in charge of her boat as she wished to be in charge of her life, and would be in charge of her own life. No Nick Rosslyon was going to run it for her. If she chose to stay when the worst was done, well that was a decision she was going to make for herself.

Suddenly the sky seemed dim, the land behind her a dreary line. As soon as she got back she was going to have to tell Millie that she had discovered the name of her father, and that he was also the grandfather of the man she loathed and who had a moral right to her beloved home, if the winning bet was to be upheld.

There seemed little doubt now that Tamar's parents had done a dishonest thing, morally dishonest at any rate. They had probably made life so difficult for their daughter that she had been forced to marry

John Polgrean to give the baby a name. Or if it had been Tamar's own choice it was one she had had to make for the baby's sake. How could they balance one wrong against another and believe they had acted correctly on both counts?

Harbour Spur was now hers, made over to her by Millie. It was her decision to work out what happened now. Suppose she didn't tell Millie about the lost wager but kept all this sordid knowledge to herself? Legally she was not obliged to do anything. It would be the easy way out. Adam would have the village his father had come to love and would make a killing financially on that no doubt. Why should he need his grand-father's money, too?

But need didn't come into it. She knew that with terrifying clarity. A wrong had been done. If she did nothing to try to right it she was as bad as Tamar Trevarrick's parents who, it seemed, had cheated Adam's grand-father out of something he had considered rightly his. And what about Millie? When she knew all there was to be known would she agree to the suppression of all the true facts so that they could keep Harbour Spur? Of course not. Her aunt was honest. Everyone knew her for an upright woman who regarded truth as of the utmost importance.

So, if she decided to go ahead and tell her aunt the truth and deprive them both of a home, should she not consider Nick's offer of marriage for the sake of her aunt? They wouldn't have any money from the sale of the house if they acknowledged Adam as the true owner. But there would be no money worries once she was married to Nick.

'Be true to yourself, Steph,' Millie was always saying. 'And then you'll always be true to other people.

She had to tell her. Then she must find Adam.

As she headed back towards land, Stephanie saw *Sea Sharon* coming out of the harbour. On board were two figures, the girl and one of the crew members. So where was Adam? Below, possibly. Now she wouldn't be seeing Adam to tell him personally. The alternative was to phone his solicitor. Millie would prefer it that way. This time everything would be done legally. Adam would inherit his grandfather's money, and no doubt invest it in the modernising of Polmerrick. That's the way it was going to be, and she must make the best of it.

Landing quickly, she pulled the boat only a short way up the shingle. The early sunlight glinted on the roofs near the harbour and on Millie's beloved hanging baskets, yellow against the white wall of Harbour Spur. Leaving the boat as it was Stephanie raced up to the house, flung open the door and crashed it shut behind her.

Ten minutes later she was back on the beach to tie up her boat securely. She didn't at first see the person standing there until she was almost upon him. He stood there in his yellow shirt and white shorts, the sunlight glinting on his dark hair. Adam? Of course it was Adam. To see him so unexpectedly made her gasp.

He stood tall and still, beside her boat, his eyes watchful.

'I thought there'd been an accident. The boat seemed abandoned.'

'I had something to do quickly,' she said. 'I had to show my aunt your grandfather's letter. I left it with her.'

And the diary, too, with only a mumbled explanation, but it was best for her aunt to study them, but on her own, quietly. She would know the significance soon enough. Millie was no fool. She had left her aunt, gasping out about seeing to the boat and that she would be back soon. At the door she had turned to kiss her aunt swiftly before running out.

'I have to tell you something, Adam,' she said, suddenly thinking of money she owed him. 'I haven't got it with me, the money for the train fare. I'm sorry I...'

He laughed.

'You think that's why I'm here?'

'Yes, no ... I don't know.'

He gave her a brilliant smile that seemed

to shine with suppressed vitality as he helped her lift the boat higher up the shingle. Before she could say anything, two strong hands took hold of hers and held them firmly. Startled, she raised her eyes to his, and at the same moment something moved in the deep recesses of her heart. She forgot everything she needed to say. Instead she gave him a sweet, loving look.

'Whatever happens, you'll have the deeds of Polmerrick,' he said.

Bewilderment flickered through her.

'Polmerrick?'

'I've made sure the village will be yours legally. It's all tied up now, yes siree. No way will I allow you to sell yourself to Nick Rosslyon. My only proviso is that Polmerrick must be in your name only, and it must remain that way. It's up to you what you do with the place. With a bit of improvement here and there I'm assured it will generate enough income to keep you comfortably independent of him. That's what I want for you, a true choice.'

Stephanie looked at him, speechless.

'Polmerrick is yours, my love, to do with as you will. I have to be sure that your decision to marry that oaf is not for financial reasons.'

He looked suddenly tense, and a muscle twitched at the side of his mouth.

'Just tell me that isn't the reason,' he concluded.

'Of course it isn't. How can it be? I'm not going to marry Nick Rosslyon.'

She knew that now for the truth. She had been mad to think of it even for a moment. It was the last thing Millie would want her to do. She should have known that all the time.

'Oh, boy, you're not?'

'Never!'

Adam smiled, and his eyes shone with a brilliance that almost blinded her. He pulled her to him and held her so tightly as he kissed her she could hardly breathe. It felt as if the sea was rising and drowning them both in a vast surge. But then she remembered the truth. She pulled away from him, gasping. Once before he had tried this approach.

She could hear his words in her mind still – *you see, Stephanie, how I need you to help me obtain the deeds of Harbour Spur.*

'What's wrong, my love? Your aunt doesn't want to sell … will never sell to me. I've had to accept that. Believe me, Stephanie.'

She turned away and began to fumble with folding the sail.

'Let me!'

She watched in silence as he did it. What she had to tell him meant that he would benefit from his grandfather's will after all. She must tell him, now. And when she did, would he be off to do what he had to do with no more thought of her than he had for one of the pebbles on the beach?

'Polmerrick, Harbour Spur – what do they matter when my love for you sets my body on fire?' he was saying, to her amazement. 'This is how my grandfather felt once for his Tazie, but he lost her. I'm not going to lose you. Come, my love.'

He held out his arms. Instinctively she fell towards him, to be gathered into his embrace.

'Emotions matter, not material things. I've learned that now, the hard way.'

His voice deepened.

'When I learned that you were to marry Rosslyon it was the worst moment of my life. It's you who matters to me, my love. You are more important to me than any money.'

Stephanie felt her hot cheeks glow.

She whispered, 'But there's another truth you have to know, about Harbour Spur and your grandfather and my grandmother.'

Her words trembled in her throat.

'There was a baby. Tazie had his baby, my aunt. I've only just found out. I ran up just now to let Millie read a letter I found behind the portrait.'

He gaped at her. Then a low whistle escaped him.

'Oh, boy!'

His eyes danced, and he let out a shout of laughter. Stephanie laughed, too, the colour warming her cheeks.

'It's not funny,' she gasped. 'But Millie said she'd give anything to know who her father was.'

'Oh, boy, I still can't believe it. Aunt Millie! What is she going to say?'

Stephanie was immediately serious.

'I shall go at once and find her.'

She had to play this right. She had no idea of Millie's reaction to her new nephew, but she was certain she would wish to play fair with him however much it hurt. But how could she doubt now that Adam loved her for herself? He was prepared to give her the deeds of Polmerrick. Was that the action of an unscrupulous rogue? Her heart knew the truth and her heart sang within her.

He released her a little and she saw the determination in his face.

'My dearest Stephanie, I want to spend the rest of my life with you. I want you to be my wife. We'll go together to tell your aunt, my aunt. If Grandfather had known he had a daughter he would want Harbour Spur to be hers, wager or no wager. I accept it. Seeing how it is, will she believe me?'

Thinking how it really was, Stephanie laughed.

'What's so funny, my dearest love?'

She wouldn't tell him yet. First she must discover her aunt's reactions to the astounding news, and pray that she would understand. Time enough for Adam to know that in exchange for the deeds of the village she would hand him the deeds of Harbour Spur. A fitting wedding present, each to the other.

'Harbour Spur,' he said softly, 'the place that meant so much to me all these years. And then I came to find it, and something else took its place in my heart. To think my search for grandfather's roots brought me to you, my love. That's success, if you like.'

Stephanie smiled, hugging her secret. Together they would do what was best for Polmerrick, for all of them. With Adam at her side she knew she now had nothing to fear.

The publishers hope that this book has given you enjoyable reading. Large Print Books are especially designed to be as easy to see and hold as possible. If you wish a complete list of our books please ask at your local library or write directly to:

Dales Large Print Books
Magna House, Long Preston,
Skipton, North Yorkshire.
BD23 4ND

This Large Print Book, for people
who cannot read normal print,
is published under the auspices of
THE ULVERSCROFT FOUNDATION